DOCTOR·WHO

The Pirate Loop

DOCTOR · WHO

The
Pirate
Loop

SIMON GUERRIER

BBC
BOOKS

2 4 6 8 10 9 7 5 3 1

Published in 2007 by BBC Books, an imprint of Ebury Publishing.
Ebury Publishing is a division of the Random House Group Ltd.

Doctor Who is a BBC Wales production for BBC One
Executive Producers: Russell T Davies and Julie Gardner
Series Producer: Phil Collinson

The Random House Group Ltd Reg. No. 954009.
Addresses for companies within the Random House Group can be found
at www.randomhouse.co.uk.

A CIP catalogue record for this book is available from the British Library.

ISBN 978 1 84607 347 2

The Random House Group Limited supports the Forest Stewardship
Council (FSC), the leading international forest certification organisation.
All our titles that are printed on Greenpeace approved FSC certified
paper carry the FSC logo. Our paper procurement policy can be found
at www.rbooks.co.uk/environment

Series Consultant: Justin Richards
Project Editor: Steve Tribe
Cover design by Lee Binding © BBC 2007

Typeset in Albertina and Deviant Strain
Printed and bound in Germany by GGP Media GmbH

For the dread pirates Luke and Joseph

Six thousand robots danced through the streets of Milky-Pink City. They had never been programmed with dance lessons but what they lacked in style they made up for with their enthusiasm. All around, metal limbs twisted with abandon. Tall robots did something that looked like a rumba, lifting robots did the Mashed Potato. And weaving in and out between them raced the Doctor and Martha Jones.

Martha and the Doctor had been in Milky-Pink City for no more than four hours and it had not gone brilliantly well. The city and all its robots had been built years ago to serve and pamper thousands of human holidaymakers, but the humans had never arrived. Intergalactic tourism, the Doctor had explained, was an unforgiving business. So the robots had been delighted to see Martha and the Doctor, even if they hadn't booked ahead. They had fallen over themselves to oblige their every whim. They squabbled about who got to fetch Martha a drink and came to blows over who took the Doctor's coat. It had quickly turned into a war between different factions of keen-to-please robots, all with exquisite manners. And then an hour later they'd turned on the Doctor and Martha as the source of all the problems.

This, thought Martha now as she ran to keep up with the Doctor, her hand held tightly in his, was what happened when you tried to force people to have a good time. She remembered a particularly miserable family holiday at some activity camp outside London, her big sister Tish falling for one of the creepy blokes that worked there. She shuddered. Even being sentenced to death by a city of daft robots wasn't quite as terrifying as that place. For one thing, you couldn't defeat creepy blokes by playing them songs from your iPod.

'It's funny,' she said to the Doctor as they ducked and weaved between the dancing robots. 'My brother hates this song.'

'What?' said the Doctor, stopping in his tracks. He spun on the heel of his trainer, his long coat and silvery tie whirling around him, and swept a hand through his spiked and scruffy hair. 'But this is a *classic*. Humans doing what you do, daring to be brown and blue and violet sky!' He laughed. 'I don't even know what that means! See? *Brilliant*.'

Martha raised an eyebrow. With the robots still dancing around them, it didn't seem the best time to indulge him.

'Yeah, well,' he said chastened, taking her hand and leading her on through the strange and metal street party, 'you know I once saw Mika live in Denmark—'

'Yeah,' said Martha wearily. 'I was there too.'

He turned his wild, inquisitive eyes on her like he'd only just noticed her there. 'That's a coincidence!' he said. 'Funny how these things work out, innit?' But his wide grin and enthusiasm were infectious; Martha found herself grinning back.

They turned a corner and Martha felt her heart leap. At the end of the alleyway, beyond yet more cavorting robots, stood the TARDIS. They made their way through the last of the dancing robots. While the Doctor rummaged through deep pockets to find the TARDIS key, Martha looked back one last time on the city. Two small robots the size and shape of kitchen bins were dancing together, the same keen but clumsy routine she remembered from old school discos. She felt a sudden pang of sorrow for the silly machines.

'But won't they get bored with this song one day?' she asked the Doctor.

'A-ha!' he said brightly, producing a yo-yo from his pocket. 'No, hang on, sorry.' He handed the yo-yo to her and had another go. 'Almost. Don't worry, I've done this before.' And he produced the innocuous-looking key. 'Yes they'll get bored,' he said as he unlocked the door to his spaceship. 'But they were programmed as holiday reps, weren't they? Every one of them's a born entertainer. They've got hooks and beats in their chips.'

Martha gaped at him. 'They'll make their own music, won't they?' she laughed. 'They'll entertain themselves.'

'Right on, sister,' grinned the Doctor. 'A bit of culture to liberate the workers. Come on, let's leave them to it.'

A moment later, with a gruff rasping, grating sound that tore through the fabric of time and space itself, the police box was gone from the alleyway. Six thousand robots lived happily ever after.

'So where next?' said the Doctor, fussing with the TARDIS controls. His long, skinny fingers danced across the strange array of instruments and dials, his face lit by the eerie pale glow from the central column.

'What about that spaceship?' said Martha.

'That spaceship,' agreed the Doctor. He began to set the coordinates, then stopped to look back up at her. 'Which spaceship?'

'That spaceship you were telling me about. When we were waiting to be executed.' She sighed and rolled her eyes. 'Just a minute ago!'

The Doctor's eyes narrowed to slits as he struggled to remember. 'Oh! *That* spaceship,' he said after a moment.

'Come on' she said, 'you said it was brilliant.'

'Well it was. Literally. The Starship *Brilliant*. Luxury passenger thing. In space. But I only told you about it to take your mind off, well, you know…' He drew a finger quickly across his neck.

'Yeah, but come on,' said Martha, leaning towards him across the console. 'You said nobody knew what happened to it. Not even you.'

'Well no,' he said, scratching at the back of his head. 'Not exactly. I mean, there are theories.' He began to step lightly around the control console, flicking switches, careful not to meet her gaze. 'It could have fallen into a black hole, or crashed into a giant space squid. You know it vanished just before a huge galactic war?'

'No,' said Martha.

'Well. That could mean something couldn't it?'

'Oh come on,' said Martha, 'you know you want to. It's a mystery!'

'Yeah, well.' The Doctor thrust a hand into the trouser pocket of his skinny, pinstriped suit; his way of looking casual. 'Exploring a spaceship that you know is going to vanish forever... Probably be a bit dangerous. Dangerous and reckless. Dangerous and reckless and irresponsible.'

'What?' she laughed. 'And never know what happened to it? Ever? That's not like you at all.'

The Doctor gazed at her, deep brown eyes open wide. Martha felt the smile on her own face falter, her insides turning over. She had come to accept that the Doctor didn't share her feelings for him, but sometimes the way he looked at her...

'So we're going?' she said quickly.

'It'll bother me if we don't,' he said, busy now with coordinates and the helmic regulator. He stopped to look back up at her. 'But there are some rules. Important ones.'

'Whatever you say.'

'Yes, *whatever I say*.' Martha did her best to look serious.

'One,' the Doctor continued. 'We can't get involved with anyone we meet. Two, we absolutely cannot change anything. Not a bean. Nuffink. Nada. Nana nee-nee noo-noo.'

'Right.'

'And three…' He turned from the controls to look at her and his eyes sparkled as he grinned. 'Oh, what's the use?' he said, and plunged the lever to send them hurtling back in time.

'Honestly, it'll be fine—' began Martha.

But the huge explosion cut her sentence short. She was thrown off her feet, hurled head over heels across the TARDIS console to crash hard into the metal mesh floor.

Typical, she thought, as everything faded to black.

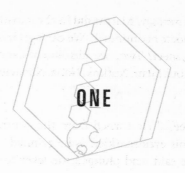

ONE

In the moment after she woke and before she opened her eyes, Martha thought she was in her mum's house in London. She could smell strong tea and cleanliness all around her as she lay sprawled on her back. Her jeans and leather jacket dug into her skin, she felt hot and heady like she'd had a late night out and the floor was trembling beneath her. Sore and a little bit fragile, she dared to look around.

Dark. Industrial. Noisy. Not the TARDIS. She closed her eyes again.

When she next awoke, she found the Doctor crouched beside her, grinning encouragingly. He brandished a chipped china mug at her with a drawing of a sheep on it.

'A little milk and no sugar, yeah?' he said.

'Ta,' she said, struggling to sit up. Her head throbbed and her limbs felt shaky, so she checked herself over for concussion. She wiggled her fingers and toes, and closed one eye and then the other to make sure her vision was OK. Everything seemed to be fine. Martha could remember the explosion in the TARDIS, being thrown off her feet and across the console, so she wasn't missing any memory. And, for all she felt battered, she didn't feel queasy, so there didn't seem to be any internal damage to worry about.

'What's the diagnosis?' asked the Doctor, with that slight, admiring smile he kept for whenever she showed a bit more intelligence than your average human ape.

'OK, I think,' she said. 'Can you check my pupils?'

He handed her the mug of tea and fished in his pocket for his sonic screwdriver. Its brilliant blue light dazzled her for a second. 'Both the same size,' said the Doctor. 'Both go all small when I shine a light at them. That's what they're meant to do, isn't it?'

'Means I'm probably not bleeding to death on the inside,' she said, batting the sonic screwdriver out of her face. 'I'm happy with that.'

So she had survived intact. And then she realised it was not a headache she could feel but the deep bass line of vast machinery thrumming all around her. They were no longer in the TARDIS. Wherever they were it stank like washing-up liquid, all efficient and clean. And it wasn't her own body that was shaking; the hard metal floor beneath her trembled with terrible power.

Martha drank the strong and pungent tea while glancing round to get her bearings. They were in the narrow alleyway between two huge machines; huge and noisy as an old factory or printing press, she thought, a whole series of sturdy great machines working flat out. She was suddenly reminded of the dark, low-ceilinged basement at the Royal Hope, where the hospital had its own power generator. Her mate Rachel had taken her down there at the end of a night shift to watch some other medical students lose at cards to the porters. Martha remembered them squeezing into a small, sweaty, claustrophobic room where you couldn't even hear yourself think. This place had the same heavy, oppressive feel to it.

'We hit the engine rooms then?' she said.

The Doctor grinned at her. 'Very good,' he said. 'Yeah, smacked right into it. Sorry. Think they must have some sort of unmentored warp core or something, and the TARDIS went a bit rabbit-in-the-headlights. Doesn't take much to turn her head these days, poor girl. I meant to put us down in the passenger lounge. Bet it's a lot more posh than this upstairs.'

'Right,' said Martha. She put down her tea and struggled unsteadily to her feet. Just along the alleyway stood the reassuring shape of the TARDIS. She could still taste the acrid smoke that had billowed from the console, and realised the Doctor must have carried her out of it, letting her down here before hurrying off to find help… and the mug of tea. The engines around her filled her head with noise and her skin felt itchy with grime. Yet the dark and solid machinery seemed immaculate; perhaps she was just imagining the dirt. She shrugged off her jacket, the air suddenly hot and clammy on her bare arms. Despite the heat, she shivered; there was something wrong about this place, she could feel it deep inside her.

And then she realised she was being watched.

There were six of them, short, stocky men wearing tough leather aprons and luridly coloured Bermuda shorts. Practical, she thought, for this hot and heavy environment. They lurked in the shadows by the machines, watching her and the Doctor nervously.

'Er, hi!' she waved at them. One of them waved back instinctively then hid his hand behind his back. The men remained where they were, skulking in the darkness.

'They're more scared of us than we are of them,' said the Doctor quietly.

'You said that in Kenya about those lions,' said Martha.

'Well, yes,' admitted the Doctor. He smiled his brightest smile as he addressed the men. 'She's feeling a lot better now, thank you. Said a tea would do the trick!'

The men remained in the shadows, watching. The Doctor nudged Martha in the ribs with a bony elbow.

'Come on,' he said, stepping forward. 'You need to thank them for the tea.'

'Right,' said Martha, feeling awkward. She hated being pushed in front of people, expected to perform. Her mum would still have important workmates round for dinner sometimes. Tish and Martha were always made to hand out the nibbles – her brother Leo always got away with filling up people's drinks. 'This is my middle one,' Mum would preen as her friends took the stuffed olives or carrot sticks and dip. 'She's going to be a leading surgeon.' It always made Martha furious, but she had never answered back. Tish, who liked playing up to her mum's image of her, said Martha had a twisted sense of duty. And Martha knew she was right. Even now, hundreds of years in the future, she felt herself adopting a familiar, joyless smile.

'Hi!' she said with badly faked delight. 'I'm Martha!' The men in the leather aprons said nothing and remained where they were. She turned to the Doctor. 'You did introduce us, didn't you?'

'Er,' said the Doctor sheepishly. 'I did call out a bit, but nobody responded. They probably didn't hear me over the noise of the engines. And then I found the kitchen and sort of helped myself. Sorry! Better leave them some coins in case they've got a tea club!' He rummaged through the pockets of his suit jacket, the inside ones first. 'Can you remember what the money is in space in the fortieth century?' Martha felt guilty; only a couple of days before she'd thrown a gold sovereign away down a wishing well.

The men in aprons seemed to cower in the darkness, and Martha realised they must think the Doctor was looking for a weapon. The poor blokes were terrified of them and she started to understand maybe why. They were the lowest of the low, toiling away in this noisy, sweaty place. They would never mix with any of the ship's passengers, and they probably only ever heard from the crew when something had gone wrong.

She reached a hand into the inside pocket of the Doctor's jacket, helping herself to the slim leather wallet that he kept with his sonic screwdriver. He raised an eyebrow at her but otherwise didn't seem to object; he liked it when she showed some initiative.

Martha flicked the wallet open, paused to picture in her mind what she wanted it to show, and then brandished it at the men still lurking in the shadows.

'There's no need for any concern,' she said, adopting the confident, reassuring tone that she'd learned from Mr Stoker. 'We're not here on an inspection. My assistant here—' she nodded her head at the Doctor '—just needs to familiarise himself with the ship's workings as part of his training. We'll just be a couple of minutes and then let you get back to your work.' She smiled her most charming smile.

The men in the Bermuda shorts and aprons turned to each other, said nothing yet seemed to confer.

'That was good,' said the Doctor quietly, taking the wallet of psychic paper from her and pocketing it carefully. Slowly, one of the men in aprons shuffled forward, glancing back to his friends, who all kept safely where they were. Martha's heart went out to the poor bloke. She thought he might have been the one who had waved before.

'That's it,' she told him. 'Me and him, we're really nothing to worry about. I'm Martha, he's the Doctor.

Who are—'

The sentence died in her throat as the man in the leather apron stepped out into the light. He was tall and muscular, his eyes alive with fear and excitement. And he didn't have a mouth.

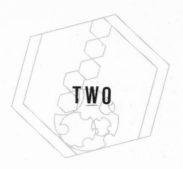

TWO

Martha realised she was staring, her own mouth hanging open. The man in the leather apron and the garish Bermuda shorts stared back at her mutely. Below the man's nose, where a mouth should have been, there was just a small, round hole, the same size as if it had been made by a hole-punch. His glistening black stubble didn't divide into beard and moustache, but covered the lower part of his face evenly. 'Right,' she said, not sure what she would say next. 'Right,' she said again.

'I think what my superior is trying to articulate,' said the Doctor, nimbly taking charge, 'is that we're very keen not to disturb what you're doing. We'll just keep out of your way.'

But the mouthless man raised his fist and began gesturing wildly. Martha grabbed the Doctor's arm to pull him back, worried he might get himself hit. The Doctor shrugged her off, and began to wave his own arm in a similarly emphatic manner.

It was some rudimentary kind of sign language.

'What's he saying?' she asked.

The Doctor and the mouthless man continued to wave their arms at each other. 'I think,' said the Doctor, 'he wants us to go that way.' He stopped waving, and pointed in the direction that the mouthless man was still indicating. The mouthless man nodded vigorously. 'Yes, I think that's what he wants.'

'Sorry,' said Martha to the mouthless man. 'But you can understand us, can't you? You can't speak but you understand English?'

The mouthless man nodded, then looked back at his colleagues. In the shadows, they nodded too. 'Oh,' said the Doctor. 'That's a good point. So, whoever you answer to, whoever gives you orders, they can tell you what to do out loud.'

Again the mouthless man nodded, and Martha felt a thrill of fear. It wasn't that this was a new species of people who just weren't born with mouths. Instead they were some kind of lower order of men, able to take instructions yet not to answer back. Either they'd been bred like this or they'd been operated on, but whatever it was they were clearly some kind of class of slaves.

Martha could see in the Doctor's eyes the same determination she felt burning hot inside herself. Whatever happened, they were going to help free these people.

The mouthless man gestured again down the passageway, beckoning the Doctor and Martha to follow him. They continued up the alley between the huge machines. The mouthless man's bare back showed strong shoulders and toned muscles, Martha noticed. His Bermuda shorts were all swirls of pink and blue.

The alley emerged into a wide, open area, about the size of Martha's tiny flat in London. The far wall was covered over with a bank of complex levers and controls. Not needing to be prompted by the mouthless man, the Doctor put on his glasses as he hurried over to inspect it.

Martha, knowing she'd make nothing of the controls herself but keen to at least look interested, headed over to a small, inset porthole to the left of all the switches. It must be some kind of inspection hatch for looking into the machine, she thought. She gazed in on a pale grey light that swirled gloopily beyond. Despite the clammy heat of the engine room she found her bare arms suddenly prickling with goose bumps. There was something scarily familiar about that grey light, but she couldn't think what it could be.

She turned to the Doctor to ask him. His mouth hung open and there was a mixture of awe and horror in his eyes.

'What?' she said.

'Oh, I'm so sorry,' he said to her softly. 'I really am.' Martha felt her heart hammering in her chest. It was what he normally said when somebody they'd met got killed.

'We're too late?' she said.

The Doctor snapped out of his reverie to look at her.

Again she saw the glimmer in his eyes, that quick and sly intelligence. 'Too late?' he said incredulously. 'Nah. It's just we've only been here five minutes and I already know what went wrong! Hate it when that happens. Well, not hate exactly. It bothers me. Brilliant word, "bothers". Like "oblong". People should use it more. Anyway, good puzzle should take an hour to solve at least. Well, with me slightly less. Like that cornfield maze on Milton Nine.'

'You got lost in that for two days,' said Martha.

'Yeah!' grinned the Doctor. 'Wasn't it brilliant? But this!' He waved a hand dismissively at the bank of controls as he turned to the mouthless man. 'Madness!' He turned back to Martha. 'You know what this is?'

Martha scrutinised the levers, dials and switches. She was acutely aware of the mouthless man watching her, and his leather-aproned colleagues still there in the shadows, too. 'Course,' she said, lying through her teeth. 'And it explains why the ship was never found, doesn't it?'

The Doctor gazed at her with the same utter bewilderment as that time she'd tried to explain about MySpace. Then his face lit up. 'Of course!' he said 'Oh, you are brilliant, Martha Jones! Brilliant!' He turned back to the controls and began to inspect the dials and readings with new-found glee.

Keen to maintain the illusion of brilliance, Martha leant in close beside him to inspect the same dials and readings. The display showed complex swirls and flourishes instead of numbers she could read.

'I think the TARDIS must have crashed quite hard,' she said. 'It doesn't translate this for me.'

The Doctor looked at her over the top of his glasses. 'Nah,' he said. 'They're not numbers as you understand them. They're expressions of atemporal mismatch. Kodicek Scale, I think.' A thought struck him. 'Are you sure you understand how this drive works?'

She shrugged. 'A bit.'

'Right,' said the Doctor. He stood up straight again, stepping away from the controls and stretching his long arms and back. He seemed about to address the mouthless man, then changed his mind and turned back to Martha. 'What bit do you understand?'

'Well,' said Martha. 'It drives the spaceship, doesn't it?'

'Aaaah,' said the Doctor, wagging a finger at her. 'But it's not a spaceship, is it?'

'Sorry. It drives the *starship*. You can be such a geek.'

'Well,' he huffed, pulling a sulky face. 'These details are important. This drive here means it doesn't travel through space.'

'What?'

'See?' he said to the mouthless man. 'She was really just winging it! Unbelievable these people. And you know what they did to the Dodo?'

The mouthless man stared at him, either not getting the joke or too wary to show that he did.

'Doctor,' said Martha levelly. 'Why don't you tell us

what this drive does.'

'Yeah, good idea,' he said. 'What we've got here is really very clever. And a good century ahead of its time. They should be on plain old hyperspace wossnames. But this? It's… it's…' he twirled a hand in the air, as if it might help conjure the right word.

'It's brilliant?' suggested Martha. Everything was brilliant with him. That's why she'd found a starship called 'Brilliant' so funny in the first place.

'Yeah,' said the Doctor, nodding. 'It's that, too. Cuts out all the boring stuff of travelling between the stars. And there's a *lot* of boring stuff out there. Billions and millions of miles of it. And empty, mostly, except for background radiation and lots of old TV. There's not a lot to do on the journey to another star. You get old, you die and you just hope your great-great-great-great-great grandkids still remember how to fly the ship.'

'Sounds fun,' said Martha.

'Oh, you lot do it with your usual pig-headed determination to do *anything* that's completely bonkers. Have I said how you're my very favourite species? But, bit of thinking, and there are ways of cutting corners.'

'Like the Time Vortex,' said Martha, who had taken some elementary lessons in how the TARDIS worked.

'Well, yeah,' the Doctor acknowledged. 'But this lot haven't got anywhere near that far yet. Which is just as well, 'cos I'd be duty-bound to stop 'em. What they've done here is to push against the surface on the outside of the Vortex. It's tough stuff, so it resists and you sort of bounce back off it. And if you can get the angle right – not that you have angles as such in nine-dimensional space – you skip along it, bump-bump-bump. I suppose it's not that graceful, now I come to think about it.'

'So it's like skimming a stone across the surface of a lake,' said Martha.

'Er, yeah,' said the Doctor. 'I wish I'd thought of putting it like that. Can we just pretend I did?'

'Yeah, whatever you like,' said Martha. 'So how does this explain how the *Brilliant* disappeared?'

'Well,' said the Doctor. 'While all the posh passengers are upstairs sipping cocktails, the ship is lurching across the surface of the space-time continuum like a stone skimming across a lake.' He beamed. 'That *is* a good analogy! And every time it presses itself into that surface, and just before it bounces back out… Well, it technically skips *out* of space and time. That's what makes it move so quickly, it misses out most of the actual distance. To anyone looking at it in just four or five dimensions, it's like it blinks out of existence.' He tried to click his fingers to demonstrate, but couldn't make them click. 'You get the idea.'

'Right,' said Martha. 'So the drive makes it flick in and out of reality, yeah?'

'Pretty much,' said the Doctor. 'Now you see me, now you don't. Now you see me again, now you don't again.'

'So it didn't blow up or fall into a black hole,' said Martha. 'It just got stuck somewhere nobody could see it.'

'Oh, I'd have been able to see it,' said the Doctor. 'If I'd gone looking.'

'Well you've got special powers, haven't you, oh mighty Last of the Time Lords?'

'Do I go on and on about that?'

Martha fluttered her eyelashes, all innocence. 'I don't think I've ever heard you mention it.'

'That's OK then. Still, it would have been a bit easier for everyone else to find it if they hadn't kept this technology quiet. I mean, I didn't know anything about this drive. Me!'

'You said there's about to be a big war, didn't you?' said Martha. 'Maybe they wanted to keep it secret from their enemies.'

'Maybe,' said the Doctor, glancing round. Martha realised he didn't want to say whatever it was he really thought while the mouthless man was still listening. But she had an idea herself; the starship's rich passengers weren't just on some wild pleasure cruise. While the rest of the galaxy was struggling not to have a war, this lot had built themselves a clever new way of escaping all the trouble.

Like she and the Doctor would be doing, if they just left in the TARDIS now. She felt awful about that, with the mouthless man stood there. They would be leaving him to his doom.

'Isn't there anything we can do for them?' she asked the Doctor quietly. 'They're going to be lost for ever, aren't they?'

The Doctor took her hand. 'You know how this works,' he said kindly. 'We can't change anything. We have to be responsible. What happens has already happened.'

'Yeah, I know,' she said. 'Still...'

'They also brought this on themselves,' said the Doctor gently. 'This drive is experimental. And they've got staff to run it who can't even tell them when it goes wrong! Oh, that's all very clever for keeping it secret, but it's also pretty stupid.' He turned to the mouthless man. 'No offence.'

The mouthless man nodded vigorously. 'See?' said the Doctor. He checked the controls again. 'Yes, see? Our friend here has sent an alert up to the captain to tell him the drive has stalled. But there's not been an answer, so presumably it hasn't got through. But at least everyone knows their place! The lowest ranks literally can't speak back to their superiors, and now that's going to cost everyone their lives.'

'It's that bad?' said Martha.

'Any effort to engage the ship with the drive stalled like this and it's likely to explode. It's really just a matter of time.'

'We have to do something!'

The Doctor reached out for her hand, gazed deep into her eyes. 'Martha, we can't. Not when it changes history.'

He gazed at her levelly with his dark and twinkling eyes. But Martha refused to look away; this was too important. She was a proper doctor, even if he wasn't.

She had a duty to stop and help. And sometimes the Doctor needed her to remind him when he was wrong.

'All right,' he said wearily. 'We'll pop upstairs. I'll have a word with the captain. A few quick pointers and then we'll let them get on their way.'

Martha grinned. 'Great!' she said. 'You know it's the right thing to do.'

'I'm not sure I do, but anyway.' He turned to the mouthless man. 'Sorry about all that yammering there,' he said. 'Just needed to parley a plan. Anyway, we're going to get this sorted out for you. Which way to the exit?'

The mouthless man again gestured wildly, using both arms this time. He seemed unable to make any noise at all, and the worst thing about it was his own frustration at not being understood.

'Maybe if you just lead us,' said Martha, trying to make it sound kind.

The mouthless man nodded. They followed him back down the alleyway between the machines, and round past the TARDIS. Set into the wall was what looked like a shower – a person-sized booth with a glass door.

'Ooh!' said the Doctor, dashing over. 'I've not seen these in years! One-way transmat up to the bridge.' He turned back to the mouthless man. 'Is it a bridge, or is it more of a cockpit?' The mouthless man shrugged, unable to reply. 'Oh, never mind,' said the Doctor, turning back to the machine. 'Martha, this is brilliant. You step inside, press the button, and *ping!* you're in a booth just like it at the far end of the ship.'

'It's a teleporter, yeah?' said Martha. 'Like in *Star Trek*.'

'Well, not *exactly* like *Star Trek*,' said the Doctor, busy trying to get the door open. It wouldn't budge. 'For one thing, it'll make a different noise. Anyway, this is just for getting upstairs without all that boring business of walking. It's cheating, if you ask me.'

'Not if you can't get into it,' said Martha.

'It's stuck!' said the Doctor, turning to the mouthless man. 'I wondered why you'd not just gone to see the captain yourself. Something must be coming through the other way. Something really, really slow. It's like being on dial-up!'

'When were you ever on dial-up?' asked Martha.

'I read about it,' said the Doctor. 'Well,' he said to the mouthless man. 'That way's blocked for the moment. Probably with some movie about a cat on a skateboard. So we'll go see your captain on Shanks's pony.'

The mouthless man stared dumbly at him.

'He means,' said Martha, 'we're going to have to walk. Why can't you talk normally?'

'What?' said the Doctor. 'And be just like everybody else?'

The mouthless man led them back round the TARDIS and then off to one side. They followed a narrow passageway to a thickly reinforced door. A complicated sequence of different handles and locks allowed the mouthless man to open it.

Martha had expected to see the plush fittings of a

luxury ship. Yet the way was barred by a strange, pale skin of material, like a kind of fungus. It totally blocked the door. The mouthless man again gestured emphatically; it was this obstacle he'd tried to explain.

'Somebody really doesn't want us getting out of here,' said the Doctor. 'Cor, this is a bit unusual!' He put his hand out and stroked the pale surface. 'Feels like cold scrambled egg!'

'Do you know what it is?' asked Martha.

'Oh yeah,' said the Doctor. 'Seen this before. The TARDIS can get clogged with the stuff.'

'It's some sort of time fungus, then?'

'That's the technical name for it, obviously,' laughed the Doctor. 'You get it where time doesn't quite meet up. Time, right, comes in chunks.'

'Chunks?' said Martha.

'Yeah,' said the Doctor. 'Really! But "chunks" sounds silly, so your lot use the Greek word *quanta*.'

'Like quantum mechanics,' said Martha.

'That's it exactly,' said the Doctor. 'So it comes in chunks. And this stuff lives in the gaps between moments, between the Planck units. Ship like this, it's going to make a lot of it. But it's weird to see it *inside* the ship.'

'It's some kind of weed?'

'Nothing like that. Something much, much, much more peculiar. You imagine you're in a lift, going between different floors.'

'This is another analogy, is it?' said Martha.

'Yes, it's another analogy. It's the only way you'll understand it! Right, you're in this lift. But it's one of those old warehouse lifts that doesn't have any doors.'

'So you see the floors going by.'

'Yeah, that's it. And when you're between floors?'

'Uh... Well, you see the bits in between the floors. Concrete and stuff.'

'Right! Now what's happened is that our little bump has stopped the ship between different floors. Only some of the ship's on one floor, and some of it's on another.'

'So this is the concrete between floors?' Martha rubbed her hand against the pale substance. Yes, it was soft and rubbery, just like cold scrambled egg.

'Yeah,' said the Doctor. 'Normally no one sees it. Which is good 'cos it doesn't half make a mess.'

'So we can't get through it, then?'

The Doctor laughed. 'What?' he said. 'When I've got this?' And he brandished his sonic screwdriver. 'I just need setting twenty-eight.' He waved the sonic screwdriver at the scrambled egg material. After a few seconds he poked the eggy skin with his finger. His fingertip broke through the surface.

'See?' he said. You just step through sharpish before it hardens again.'

'It's that simple?' said Martha, not wholly convinced.

'Trust me,' said the Doctor.

She laughed. 'You know you only say that when it's really bad.'

'Do you want me to go first?'

That was enough to decide her. 'No,' she said. 'You can cover my back.'

THREE

It took a while for the sonic screwdriver to soften the stuff blocking the door. Martha had time for another cup of tea and a one-sided chat with the mouthless man in Bermuda shorts and leather apron. It seemed brilliant at first that she could tell him anything and all he could do was listen. But the unfairness of it soon got to her. She had told him all about her family, and Dad and Annalise, and she didn't know one tiny thing about the mouthless man himself. Did he like his job? Did he have someone who loved him? He just watched her, nodding encouragingly but not even able to smile.

Again she felt that fierce determination to do something for these people. Somehow, she and the Doctor were going to make things better.

'Right,' said the Doctor, prodding the scrambled egg with his fingers. 'Think that's soft and squidgy.'

'How thick is it?' asked Martha, suddenly rather nervous.

'Er... No idea,' said the Doctor. 'I've never done this before. Can't be too thick if it resonates so quickly. But who knows?'

'That's not exactly reassuring.'

'No? Well, I'll be along right after you. We can compare notes on the other side.'

'OK,' she said, not feeling very much better. She took a deep breath and braced herself, like this was a fairground ride.

'And don't wander off,' said the Doctor.

She stuck her tongue out at him and walked boldly right into the strange material.

The scrambled egg material closed tightly around her, cold and rubbery and awful. Martha pushed on through.

She emerged blinking into a narrow corridor, all dark and varnished wood, with plush, red carpet underfoot. You could tell there had been money spent on it, sure, but the corridor felt cramped and not very extravagant. Someone as tall as the Doctor would have trouble standing up straight.

There was none of the eggy material on her – she was entirely clean. She glanced briefly up and down the corridor to check nobody was coming. Martha itched to explore further but she knew that the moment she did the Doctor would pop through the scrambled egg behind her and only roll his eyes. So she settled down on the floor to wait for him. Her back rested against the smooth, hard wood. She checked her watch; it was a little after two in the morning. Time didn't mean much when you travelled with the Doctor.

The floor and walls vibrated gently with power, and in the pit of her stomach Martha could feel that the ship was moving. She pressed a hand against the skin of scrambled egg that blocked the way back into the engine rooms. It felt warm and slightly sticky, but it did not yield.

She shivered with sudden fear. Of course, she thought, there just wasn't any way that she could be separated from him for ever. If the door didn't work, he could use the teleporter thing. Whatever it took, the Doctor would find a way back to her. She had complete faith in that.

But it was still taking him ages. Martha found that she was bored. 'Come on,' she told the wall of cold scrambled egg. 'I'll give you five minutes and then I'm going to explore.'

'Are you quite well, madam?' said a voice she didn't know.

Martha looked round quickly, to see her own face reflected back at her. She looked a little surprised.

'I do beg your forgiveness,' said the polished metal robot, backing away from her smoothly. His tone made it sound as if when he spoke he was also raising one eyebrow, as if it were all her fault. He wasn't like the robots of Milky-Pink City; while they had been all keen-to-please, he sounded well-schooled and sarcastic. Martha looked him quickly up and down.

'You're some kind of waiter?' she said.

'Really, madam, you're too kind,' said the robot drolly. 'I am a starship's steward.'

'Course you are,' said Martha, getting quickly to her feet. The robot made no move to assist her. He was a bit shorter than she was and even skinnier, his chrome surfaces sparkling brightly. And she found him somehow unsettling. It took a moment for her to realise that he hadn't been built to seem like a man in a suit. Not even the Doctor with his skinny arms and legs could fit inside so slender a body. The robots of Milky-Pink City had been built with bigger bones, so as not to freak out the humans.

'Might I enquire as to your berth number, madam?' the robot asked her wearily. She got the feeling it spent a lot of time rounding up lost passengers.

'My what?' said Martha. 'Sorry, I'm new around here.'

Somewhere off in the distance, Martha felt sure she heard a crash. Not a crash like the ship changing gear or anything. A crash like something going wrong.

The robot didn't seem to notice, though. It stared at her with unmoving, metal eyes.

'Your berth number, madam,' it repeated. 'It will be on your key-fob and on the door to your berth.'

'Oh!' said Martha. 'Like my room number?'

'Indeed, madam,' said the robot.

'Oh, well, I'm not—' She was about to say that she wasn't a passenger, but had a sudden thought. 'What do you do with stowaways round here?'

The robot stood up a little straighter. 'Checking,'

he said. After a moment that seemed to suggest it had delved through a vast bank of memory, it continued: 'There is no precedent for dealing with stowaways aboard the *Brilliant*, madam. Yet the regulations state that our first priority is to our passengers' safety. So in such an instance the crew are authorised in the use of deadly force.'

'Right,' said Martha. 'You'd kill them?'

'We would be authorised to do so. Might I enquire as to your berth number, madam?'

'Oh, right,' she said. 'It's Twenty-Eight.' That was the sonic screwdriver setting the Doctor had used on the scrambled egg. Maybe it was lucky.

'Checking,' said the robot.

Martha waited for it to conclude that she was a liar and a threat to the passengers. She couldn't see if it had any weapons, but perhaps it fired lasers out of its eyes. Martha had met a couple of species who could do stuff like that.

'I do apologise, Ms Malinka,' said the robot. 'I shall remember your name from now on.'

'That's OK,' said Martha nervously. 'But really, call me Martha.'

'As you wish, Ms Martha,' said the robot.

Again there was a crash from somewhere else on the ship, possibly upstairs. It definitely wasn't anything good. Again the robot seemed not to notice. Martha gave it the benefit of the doubt, worried that if she started asking questions she'd make the robot suspicious.

'And have you got a name?' she said. 'Since we're being all informal.'

The robot bowed. 'My designation is "Gabriel".'

'Hello, Gabriel,' said Martha easily. 'Glad we got that sorted.'

'Indeed, Ms Martha,' said Gabriel. He seemed to be waiting for something. Martha couldn't think what it was. She found it unnerving being watched at the best of times, but this bloke, with his impossibly skinny body and a head that worked like a mirror, was really something else.

'What?' she said.

'Might I get you an aperitif, Ms Martha?' said Gabriel.

'That'd be nice,' said Martha. 'What have you got?'

'It might be best were you to accompany me to the cocktail lounge, Ms Martha. Then you can choose from our extensive menu.'

'Ah,' said Martha. 'Thing is, I'm waiting on this bloke.'

'I am programmed with discretion parameters, Ms Martha,' said Gabriel.

'No! Nothing like that! You're as bad as my mum.'

'I do apologise, Ms Martha.'

'He's just this bloke. Nothing special. Nothing, you know... And I'm meant to wait for him.' She grinned. 'Could you just go and fetch me a cocktail?'

'I regret we are not advised to encourage passengers to take drinks out of the cocktail lounge, Ms Martha.'

'It's a health and safety thing, is it?'

The third crash was much more noticeable; the whole ship lurched under their feet. Martha collided with the very hard, dark wood of the wall. Gabriel swayed expertly in time with the lurching, and remained coolly on his feet.

'No, Ms Martha,' he said. 'They might spill them.'

'And that would make a mess of your lovely carpets, I suppose,' she said.

'More importantly, it would inconvenience the passengers, Ms Martha.'

Martha sighed. It wasn't merely that she'd said she wouldn't wander off. After all, the Doctor would expect her to use her initiative. Especially since, with all these crashes, there had to be something going on. But things always had to be so complicated, didn't they? She wanted to ask the robot what that was all about, but feared it might show she wasn't a passenger. And then the robot might kill her.

So she had to go along with him, though she had no way to tell the Doctor where she had got to. Martha had never really been one for handbags, mostly because she kept losing them, but right now a pen and a bit of paper would have been quite useful.

'If I might make a suggestion, Ms Martha,' said Gabriel. 'Once you have accompanied me to the cocktail lounge, I would be happy to return here. I could wait on the gentleman and explain to him where you are.'

'Well, yeah, that'd be good,' said Martha. But she had been with the Doctor long enough to know a trap when she saw one. 'Why are you so keen to get me into this cocktail lounge?'

The robot had a smooth, expressionless face and yet still contrived to look guilty. 'I apologise for any perceived subterfuge, Ms Martha,' he said.

'And if I refuse to go with you?'

'Checking,' said Gabriel. 'The regulations state that our first priority is our passengers' safety. So in such an instance I would be authorised to escort you by force.'

'I see,' said Martha. 'So I don't really have any choice, do I?'

This didn't seem to have occurred to Gabriel. 'Checking,' he said. He checked for a moment and then admitted dourly, 'No, Ms Martha.'

Martha tried to remember the route as they made their way to the cocktail lounge. They turned left, left again and then right, and then made their way up a wide staircase. The ceilings were higher on this new level but it still felt cramped and claustrophobic.

Gabriel led Martha into a lavish ballroom, a vast space after the narrow corridors, but still small and claustrophobic. Loud and laughing voices came from somewhere beyond.

Two rows of slender columns divided the room in three. The columns, reaching from floor to ceiling, suggested that such a wide, open space threatened the integrity of the ship. Martha had already learnt that space travel was never as glamorous and clean as it looked on telly. Yet when the Doctor had told her about the *Brilliant* before, she'd imagined something slightly less difficult. Something glamorous and a bit posh. This was more like a rickety old crate with nice carpet.

Another robot packed up tables and stacked them in a corner; Martha had clearly missed dinner. It all just got better and better.

Gabriel did not seem to acknowledge this other robot as he led Martha past. She resisted the urge to help with the tables. But as she crossed the room, she could see the carpet glittering with broken glass. Now she looked, one of the tables had been smashed apart, too; the robot stacked broken pieces. Again, the robots declined to acknowledge whatever had happened. Martha felt a sudden need to run, though she knew she had nowhere to go. Besides, the voices coming from the next room sounded lively and friendly.

Beyond the ballroom, and through a discreet door, the small cocktail lounge awaited. Her nostrils flared at a sudden tang of oranges and lemons. For a moment she thought the lounge must be perfumed, but as she stepped through the door she realised the sweet stench came from the tentacled aliens.

There were maybe a dozen of them, tubby, egg-shaped creatures, either all-orange or all-pale-blue. They crowded around the great bay window, looking out onto twinkling stars. Martha realised they were right at one end of the ship, where the passengers could sip elegant drinks and admire the view. Their ball gowns looked expensive and floaty, and they wore lots of heavy jewellery all down their long and nimble tentacles. Martha watched them busy with chatting and drinking, and ignoring her arrival. For all she couldn't name the species, she felt like she must have seen them before. And then it struck her: it was like going to a party with Mr Tickle's family.

'Hello!' she said brightly, like her sister did at parties. The aliens stopped talking to look at her. There was a sudden, horrible silence.

'Er...' said Martha. She hated being the centre of attention. And these aliens had big, staring eyes. It didn't help that she knew their posh party through the stars depended on those sorry, mouthless men, slaving away downstairs.

'Might I get you an aperitif, Ms Martha?' said Gabriel. The party of aliens clearly took this to mean they could carry on with their urgent conversations. Martha was again ignored. She couldn't thank Gabriel enough.

'That'd be nice,' said Martha. 'What have you got?'

Another robot manned the long bar on one side of the lounge. The menu offered all kinds of brightly coloured drinks that Martha had never heard of. The only thing she recognised on the list was 'hydrogen hydroxide' – or water, as they called it back home. Martha could have it in a glass, in a bowl or in an 'immature Mim'. She thought she could live without knowing exactly what that last one was.

She sipped her water, feeling under-dressed in her

jeans and vest-top, and terribly tall and awkward around the dumpy aliens. It was no fun being so noticeable at a party; it made her all self-conscious. She just wanted to be invisible. Slowly, Martha made her way to the great bay window and looked out into the darkness beyond. The stars seemed tiny, so distant that she couldn't tell if the ship were moving towards them or away. Perhaps one of those tiny pinpricks of light was her own sun. Or perhaps she was too far from home even for that. She would never get used to that feeling.

'And what do you make of it all, dear?' asked an orange alien beside her, so suddenly Martha spilt her glass of water.

'Oh, I'm sorry,' said Martha, feeling even more stupid as other aliens turned to look at her.

'No, no,' said the alien, kindly. 'We're all a little unnerved. I'm Mrs Wingsworth. My friends call me Mrs Wingsworth.'

'I'm Martha,' said Martha, holding out her hand.

Mrs Wingsworth peered at it suspiciously. 'Is there something the matter with your paw?' she asked.

'No,' laughed Martha. 'It's a custom on my planet. We shake hands when we make friends.' She slowly reached for the tip of Mrs Wingsworth's right tentacle and showed her how it was done. The tentacle felt rough and wrinkled, like an elephant's trunk.

'How marvellous!' laughed Mrs Wingsworth. 'I must remember that for my brother. He's a great enthusiast for primitive cultures.'

'My pleasure,' said Martha, though she didn't feel it. Last time she'd been so patronised she'd been washing floors in a school. 'So what are people unnerved about? Is something going on?'

'My dear!' said Mrs Wingsworth, wrapping a tentacle around her in what Martha realised was meant to a friendly manner. 'I'm afraid,' said Mrs Wingsworth gleefully, like this was *such* an adventure, 'that our vessel has been invaded!'

'What?' said Martha. 'By who?'

'By,' teased Mrs Wingsworth, taking her time to explain, 'aliens! It's thrilling, isn't it?'

Martha wished she had asked for something stronger than a glass of water. Of course there'd be an alien invasion somewhere. There always was when the Doctor showed up.

'What kind of aliens?' she said.

'You'll be able to see in a minute. They're making their way down here. Probably want to kill a few of us!' Mrs Wingsworth seemed to find the whole thing delicious fun.

Martha extracted herself from the long orange tentacle and made her way over to Gabriel. 'Has the *Brilliant* been invaded?' she asked the robot.

'I'm afraid so, Ms Martha,' said Gabriel. 'They gave orders that passengers should all remain in this room, and that they would kill anyone who left it.'

'That's why you brought me here, then?' Martha asked Gabriel. 'It was for my own safety.'

'Indeed, Ms Martha.'

'Oh, we'll be perfectly all right, dear,' said Mrs Wingsworth. 'So long as we do as we're told.'

'But Gabriel! The Doctor will walk right into them,' she said. 'The bloke I was waiting for, I mean.'

'I shall return to the engine room and intercept him,' said Gabriel. 'Please do not worry yourself, Ms Martha.'

He turned to go, and Martha ordered a refill of water from his colleague behind the bar. A gasp of excitement from the other passengers made her turn quickly round.

Three burly, humanoid spacemen stood in the doorway to the cocktail lounge, chunky-looking guns in their hands. Their faces were hidden by dark, domed space helmets. A skull and crossbones had been crudely painted on the chests of their battered spacesuits: they were pirates.

'You there,' snarled one of them gruffly, jabbing his gun towards Gabriel. They had just blocked his way out of the cocktail lounge. The robot bowed his head curtly.

'Requests by passengers take precedence over—' he began. The pirate shot him without a second thought and Gabriel vanished in a flash of blinding pink light. Several of the alien passengers screamed. When the light died away, there was nothing left to see of Gabriel – he had been completely obliterated. Martha had learned to keep silent, but still she felt utterly bereft; that had been her fault.

'Right then, you 'orrible lot,' the pirate addressed

them. 'No one else 'ere leaves the room. Not even t'go to the toilet.'

The other pirates had positioned themselves round the cocktail lounge strategically, and seemed satisfied that they now held the room. Martha could only keep any two of them in her line of vision at once. The pirate who had shot the robot nodded at his colleagues, and each pirate in turn worked the controls at the necks of their spacesuits. There was a hiss of air as the suits depressurised, and then the robot-killer took off his helmet.

Martha gasped. She glanced back round at the other pirates, who were also removing their helmets. They were the same species. Each pirate wore a thick gold earring in his left ear, so heavy it made the ear droop. They each had the same twin black stripes running down their hairy faces, hiding mischievous, twinkling eyes. And it took Martha a moment to realise what she was looking at.

The pirates. They were badgers.

FOUR

'**Y**ou're not Martha Jones,' said the Doctor as he stepped out of the scrambled egg membrane that blocked the door to the engine room.

'No, Mr Doctor,' said the slender machine in the shape of a flight steward. It bowed its head politely.

'Well hello anyway,' said the Doctor, clicking off his sonic screwdriver, spinning it in the air and then deftly dropping it into the inside pocket of his suit. He then banged his head on the dark wooden ceiling. 'Cramped in here, innit?' he said. 'Reminds me a bit of the SS *Great Britain*. I helped lay a carpet on that. You're a Bondoux 56, aren't you?'

'Indeed, Mr Doctor,' said the machine. 'Though I have been remodelled for this voyage with the latest accoutrements.'

'Good for you,' grinned the Doctor. 'I was gonna say you were a bit old-fashioned for the fortieth century, even when it's all retro like this place. But these accoutrements of yours. They don't half look like they hurt.'

The machine bent to examine its own battered body. The once highly polished chrome of its chest was smeared purple and black where it had been charred by flame. One slender arm still retained its original, elegant shape, the other had been badly twisted by the fire. The machine hesitated, as if it couldn't think quite what to say. It'd probably have protocols that stopped it slagging off the passengers or crew, thought the Doctor. So if one of them had done this, it would find it hard to say so.

'You don't have to tell me if you don't want to,' said the Doctor kindly.

The Bondoux 56 stood stiffly upright, and was probably in need of an oil. The Doctor would just find out where Martha was, have a word with the *Brilliant*'s captain and then maybe they could do a quick repair; he really liked to be fixing things. 'There was…' said the machine, and hesitated. It took a full second before it selected the right word. 'An altercation, Mr Doctor. It is of no consequence.'

'Well that's very brave of you,' said the Doctor. 'Now, you seem to know who I am, so I'm guessing you've met my friend Martha.'

'Indeed, Mr Doctor. I have had that pleasure.'

'She is nice, isn't she?' said the Doctor. 'Clever and able and she's got lovely hair. Mind you, she likes to talk back to those older and more experienced, but I was the same at her age. She'll grow out of it by the time she's 300. Where can I find her?'

'The last time I saw Ms Martha she was in the cocktail lounge, Mr Doctor,' said the machine.

The Doctor laughed. 'I might have known. "Don't wander off," I say, and the moment she's out of sight it's "I'll have a white wine spritzer!"'

'Begging your pardon, Mr Doctor, but Ms Martha ordered a measure of hydrogen hydroxide. In liquid form.'

'The scamp! I can't believe she's found a bar *and* got served in less than thirty seconds.'

'Begging your pardon, Mr Doctor?'

A terrible thought struck the Doctor. His eyebrows pressed together as he scrutinised the machine. 'How long's it been since you saw her?' he asked.

'Checking,' said the machine. 'It has been three hours, forty-two minutes and… eighteen seconds since I last saw Ms Martha.'

'What!' said the Doctor. 'Three hours, forty-two minutes and… twenty-three seconds? Really? You mean Martha was in the cocktail lounge three hours, forty-two minutes and… twenty-nine seconds ago?'

'Indeed, Mr Doctor,' said the machine.

'Well that's clever of her. It only felt like thirty seconds to me. And I'm usually very good at that sort of thing. Being the last of the—' He grinned, sheepishly. 'Oh, never mind.'

He turned to examine the membrane of scrambled egg blocking the way back into the engine room, prodding it with a finger. It felt soft and warm and rubbery, but didn't yield to him. He buzzed the sonic screwdriver at it, on setting twenty-eight. Nothing. Settings twenty-nine and forty-one did no good either.

'Hmm,' he said, turning back to the machine. 'That's a bother. So it only *felt* like thirty seconds to me since Martha stepped through, but it's really been three hours, forty-three minutes and… eleven seconds. Approximately.'

'Begging your pardon, Mr Doctor,' said the machine. 'I do not understand.'

'Ah well,' said the Doctor. 'There's this experimental drive in there,' he indicated the eggy doorway with his thumb. 'And it's stalled or something, so the engine room is now cut off in a separate pocket of time. Like the engine room and the rest of the ship are running at different speeds. Which, now I think about it, is why it was so difficult to land here.'

The Bondoux 56 considered this. 'Begging your pardon, Mr Doctor,' it said. 'I do not understand.'

'Well, that's all right, it *is* a bit complicated,' said the Doctor. 'The engine room is running at a different speed to us out here, so when you're in there it's like everything out here is moving really, really fast. Voosh! And out here, it's like everything in there is moving really, really slowly. Like how time stretches out in that bit after lunch break and before it's home time.'

The Bondoux 56 bowed its head. 'Begging your pardon, Mr Doctor,' it began. The Doctor interrupted.

'Never mind that,' he gabbled. 'This is more for my own benefit. It's because they're moving at different speeds that you get this skin of scrambled egg between the two. And it means you can only pass one way through it. Why's that, you say? Well, because… um… I know! You can only speed up in one direction. Obvious, really, 'cos otherwise you're speeding *down*. And I guess that great big download waiting in the transmat machine in there is someone from this side transmatting down at normal speed.' His eyes widened in horror. 'I hope whoever's in there doesn't notice the delay. That could be pretty nasty.' He clapped his hands together. 'Never mind. Nothing we can do about it just now, is there? I'll have to work out how we get back in there somehow, but first things first I always say. So what's next? What have I missed?' He addressed the machine. 'What's Martha told you?'

'She said, "But Gabriel! The Doctor will walk right into them,"' said the Bondoux 56, doing quite a good impression of Martha's London accent. 'I volunteered to meet you.'

'Gabriel?' said the Doctor. 'She called you Gabriel?'

'Indeed, Mr Doctor.'

'That's her name for you?' he laughed.

'I regret it is my designation, Mr Doctor.'

The Doctor realised he'd been rude – which was good, as he normally needed other people to point that out to him. Probably Martha's influence, he thought. He patted the machine fondly on its less burnt shoulder. 'Oh, don't say that. It's a nice name, Gabriel. If I remember rightly, it means you're here to help us. And are you here to help us?

'Indeed, Mr Doctor,' said Gabriel. 'My function is to serve the passengers.'

'And I bet you do it brilliantly. What did Martha want you to warn me about?'

Gabriel considered. 'Ms Martha did not ask me to warn you about anything, Mr Doctor. I said I would escort you to the cocktail lounge.'

'Right,' said the Doctor. 'I'm going to walk into a "them" some time, but so long as there's nothing you should be telling me.'

'Checking,' said Gabriel. 'Might I enquire as to your berth number, Mr Doctor?'

'My what?' said the Doctor. 'Oh, I'm not a passenger. I'm just helping out.'

Gabriel considered this new fact. 'I have nothing I should be telling you, Mr Doctor,' it said.

'OK,' said the Doctor warily, sure he was missing out on something important. But he had things to be getting on with: find Martha, then find the *Brilliant*'s captain, then work out a way of getting back into the engine rooms, and then – if the ship hadn't blown up by that point – see what he could do to fix Gabriel. 'Come on,' he said. 'You'd better take me to this cocktail lounge.'

Gabriel led the way along the corridor. They turned left, left again and then right, and up a wide staircase into a dining room where the ceiling was a little higher and the Doctor could stand up straight. Two rows of columns held up the low ceiling. An area at the far end of the room was free of columns, which probably allowed for dancing. Stood in this space, definitely not dancing, were two badger-faced people in spacesuits.

The Doctor had met a lot of different species, but he couldn't remember any that looked quite so like humans with badger faces. Which meant, what with the mouthless men downstairs and all, that he could make some educated guesses about what sorts of creature they must be. It helped in working out what they might be doing aboard the *Brilliant* that the badgers each wore a thick gold earring in their left ears, both had a skull and crossbones crudely painted on the chests of their battered spacesuits and both brandished heavy space guns. The fortieth century had quite a vogue for old-school piracy in space, recalled the Doctor. Badger-faced ones were just a bit more distinctive than the ones he'd encountered before.

'Hiyah!' he said to them, keen to appear friendly. 'Have I missed tea?'

'Thought Dash'd done for this one already, Archie,' said one of the badgers. She had a gruff but female voice, and a noticeable accent. Maybe Home Counties. Maybe even Hampshire. Perhaps just down the road from Romsey. The Doctor realised she wore pastel pink lipstick around her hairy, snarly mouth.

'Thought Dash'd done for it an' all, Joss,' said the other badger, raising his heavy space gun. He had the same accent, more broad Southampton than like pirates in old movies.

'Hang on a tick—' began the Doctor. But he was

too late. Archie shot Gabriel squarely in the chest, and Gabriel disappeared in a ball of pink light. When the light died away, there was nothing left to see of Gabriel, just a metallic tang in the air – he had been completely obliterated. 'That was a bit…' began the Doctor, tailing off as the two badgers pointed their heavy space guns at him. He tried a disarming, goofy smile. 'Wasn't it?'

'What are you, then?' said Archie the badger space pirate.

'Me?' said the Doctor. 'Oh, I'm no one important.' He grinned. 'Well, we're all important, aren't we? But I mean, I'm nobody you want to worry about.'

'Can I kill 'im?' Archie asked Joss gruffly. His wet, black nose twitched with excitement.

'He doesn't have to, you know,' the Doctor told her. 'I might have skills. Or know stuff.'

'What sort of stuff?' said Joss. The Doctor wondered what that name was short for. He'd once been good friends with a Josephine.

'Oh, you know,' he said. 'I can do tricks. Make stuff. I know a few jokes.'

'Aw,' said Archie excitedly. 'Go on, tell us a joke!'

'OK,' said the Doctor.

'A clean one,' warned Joss.

'Oh,' said the Doctor. 'OK. Um…' He racked his brains. 'Ha! Got one. Why are pirates called pirates?'

Archie and Joss conferred in whispers before they both shrugged at each other. 'We don't know,' said Joss. 'Why are pirates called pirates?'

The Doctor beamed. 'Because they ahhhhr!' he said.

The two badgers stared at him. 'I don't get it,' said Archie, scratching his head with a hairy paw. 'Can I kill 'im yet?'

'I've got other jokes,' said the Doctor quickly. 'Funny ones.'

'Not jus' yet, Archie,' said Joss. 'We wanna know where 'e's come from, don't we?'

'Yeah,' leered Archie. 'Where'd ya come from?'

'Just, er, back there,' said the Doctor, pointing to the stairs.

'There wasn't no one down there when we looked before,' said Joss.

'I was sort of hiding,' said the Doctor. 'I thought it was a game.'

'It weren't no game!' snarled Archie. Then he turned back to Joss. 'Was it?'

Joss considered. 'I reckon,' she said, 'this gent shows us where 'e was hiding. And if we don't like what 'e's got to show us, then you get to kill him.'

'Yeah!' said Archie eagerly.

'Yes, that does seem entirely fair, doesn't it?' said the Doctor. He stuck his hands into his trouser pockets. 'Well you might as well follow me, then.'

Ignoring the way they prodded him with their guns, the Doctor led them back down the stairs, left, right and right again into the passageway that ran past the door to the engine rooms. He had to stoop because of the low ceiling, and his mind was a whirl of thoughts and stratagems. He'd already worked out a couple of ways by which he might escape, but he needed to know what these pirates were after. So it was time to test a theory. 'Here we are,' he said.

'What's this?' asked Joss warily as she looked at the membrane that blocked the doorway.

'It feels like scrambled egg, doesn't it?' said the Doctor.

'Scrambled what?' said Joss.

'Egg,' said the Doctor. 'It's what chickens come in.'

'He means packaging,' Joss explained to Archie as they both sniffed and pawed the eggy material. 'Yeah, I guess it is like that.'

'And I was in there,' said the Doctor. 'Hiding. Like I said.'

'Huh,' said Joss. 'Anyone else in there?'

'Just some engineers. It *is* the engine rooms. They won't give you any trouble.'

The badgers' eyes lit up at this, just as he thought they might if they were here to pinch the experimental drive. Joss thumped the skin of scrambled egg with the end of her gun, a blow that should have done real damage. She might be a lady badger, thought the Doctor, but she could hold her own with the boys. Yet despite the force of the blow, the skin of scrambled egg did not yield.

'How'd you get through it?' she said.

'Er, you don't,' said the Doctor. 'You can only go through one way. From that side to this.'

'Hmm,' said Joss. 'It's got to be some kind of barricade.

We'd better tell Dash about this,' she told Archie.

'Yeah,' said Archie. He aimed his gun at the scrambled egg and fired two blasts. The skin fizzed with pink light for barely an instant, but was otherwise completely unharmed. 'Bah,' said Archie. 'That's no fun.'

'So we should tell Dash, then?' suggested the Doctor, just to get things moving.

'Yeah,' said Joss. 'Good idea.' These badgers, thought the Doctor, weren't exactly the brightest species he'd ever encountered on his travels. Yet Joss was eyeing him warily, her dark eyes hidden by the twin black stripes down her face. It made her expression difficult to read, but the Doctor could see a wily, predatory cunning. She might not be an intellectual, but Joss could well mean trouble.

'What?' he said, as innocently as he could.

'There's people still in there,' she said.

'Yeah,' said the Doctor.

'An' they can get out an' we can't get in.'

'Yeah.'

'S'not fair,' she said.

The Doctor nodded kindly. 'Life often isn't,' he said. 'It's one of those things.'

'What we gonna do, Joss?' asked Archie.

Joss considered, scratching her hairy chin with a paw. 'We gotta even things up a bit,' she said. She ushered Archie and the Doctor back along the passageway towards the ballroom. Then she turned and fired her gun at the ceiling above the door to the engine room.

She kept her claws on the trigger, so that a sustained burst of pink energy crashed into the woodwork. Wisps of smoke began to curl from the ceiling. Then there was a flicker of bright flame –

And shumm!

A heavy metal fire door crashed down in front of them, blocking their view of the corridor.

'Ooh, clever,' cooed the Doctor. He wrapped at the fire door with a knuckle. It bonged with a low, heavy note. 'The fire doors have locked off the corridor, so no one can get through.'

'None can get in,' agreed Joss. 'And none can get out. S'fair that way.'

'A stalemate,' said the Doctor.

'Speak for yourself,' warned Archie, prodding him with his gun.

'Them engineers will 'ave to eat some time,' said Joss. 'We'll let 'em get 'ungry and then we talk terms.'

The Doctor thought it best not to explain about the time difference in the engine room; the badger pirates could starve the engineers for days and days, but to the engineers themselves it would only seem like a few hours. He also wondered if the engineers ate food, what with their having no mouths. Perhaps they just plugged themselves into the mains, so that blocking the door wouldn't bother them.

'Right,' said the Doctor. 'Well that was fun. Now I was going to have a word with the captain, and then I thought I'd—'

Joss poked him with her gun. 'You're not leaving my sight, starshine,' she told him.

'OK,' said the Doctor, gently moving the gun aside so that it didn't point right at him. 'You drive. So where are we going?'

'You're gonna sit in the bar wiv' all the uvva prisoners,' said Joss.

'That sounds very sociable,' said the Doctor. He was itching to find out if Martha was OK, so there didn't seem much point in protesting.

Archie and Joss escorted him back up the corridor, left, left again and then right, and up the wide staircase into the dining room. They passed through the door at the back of the room into the small cocktail lounge. Another gruff-looking badger pirate guarded about a dozen egg-shaped, tentacled Balumin prisoners, who huddled in front of the great bay window that looked out on to the Ogidi Galaxy. Martha was nowhere to be seen. The Doctor bit his lip. If the badgers didn't hold her prisoner, she might still be hiding somewhere. He didn't want to get her in trouble by asking if they'd seen her.

'This is cosy,' he said. 'You must be Dash. Joss and Archie have been telling me all about you.'

The third badger pirate leered at him. He had the same gold earring in his left ear, and the same skull and crossbones on the chest of his spacesuit. He seemed older and surlier than his two comrades.

'Aye,' he leered, with the same gruff Hampshire accent. 'And who are you?'

Archie nudged Joss in the ribs. 'We never asked his name!' he said.

'That's OK,' said the Doctor. 'You had more important things to worry about. Hello. I'm the Doctor. I'm not important. Not in that way, anyway. How's everybody here?'

The Balumin murmured quietly that they were mostly fine. For all they were being held prisoner, they looked rather at home. They wore the latest fashions and held pretty drinks in their tentacles. If anything, it was the three badger pirates who looked totally out of place. The cocktail lounge was a place for wearing ties.

Joss explained to Dash about the door to the engine room. Dash listened keenly, all the time watching the Doctor. The Doctor tried not to notice; Dash seemed the brightest of this bunch. While the badgers talked about him, the Doctor wandered over to the Balumin prisoners.

'You're sure everyone is all right?' he said. They tutted and said they were fine, rather rudely. All right, thought the Doctor, you can rescue yourselves.

A bright orange Balumin woman of late middle age came over, offering him a plate of cheese and pineapple on sticks.

'Thanks very much,' he said, taking two sticks at once. 'Can't remember the last time I had these.'

'I'm Mrs Wingsworth,' the Balumin lady explained, not nearly as rudely as the other passengers. 'You'll be Martha's friend the Doctor.'

'Silence!' roared Dash from across the room.

The Doctor said nothing but nodded at Mrs Wingsworth. She only laughed and rolled her large eyes.

'Oh, don't worry yourself about these poor lambs, dear,' she said, fluttering a tentacle at the badgers. 'They're just a bit of a nuisance.'

'I'm warning you,' growled Dash, pointing his gun at her.

'See what I mean, dear?' said Mrs Wingsworth lightly, again offering the plate of cheese and pineapple sticks to the Doctor. 'Have another of these. You look like you need filling up.'

'I really don't think you should antagonise them,' the Doctor told her. 'They've got big guns and stuff like that.'

'Oh, I know!' she said. 'It really is such a bore.'

Dash stalked over to prod Mrs Wingsworth with a hairy paw.

'What you call me?' he seethed.

'I'm sure she didn't mean it,' said the Doctor gently. Dash turned to him angrily, but the Doctor held his gaze. After a moment, Dash's shoulders sagged.

'We're not boars, we're badgers,' he said.

'I know that,' said the Doctor. 'I'll tell her.'

'Good.' Dash glared at Mrs Wingsworth, then shuffled back to his comrades.

'You need to be careful,' the Doctor told Mrs Wingsworth quietly. And she laughed, loudly so the badgers would hear. The Doctor thought she might even have done it on purpose.

'But they really *are* such bores!' she said.

'What!?' roared Dash.

'Now wait—' said the Doctor.

'Oh they are,' said Mrs Wingsworth. 'You know they are.'

'Right,' said Dash, raising his heavy gun at her.

'She didn't mean it,' said the Doctor.

'Oh, I did, dear!' laughed Mrs Wingsworth.

'No, don't!' said the Doctor.

Too late. Dash fired the heavy gun and Mrs Wingsworth was soon engulfed in the dazzling pink light. She just had time to roll her eyes wearily at the Doctor and say, 'You see?'

Then the light consumed her utterly.

FIVE

More than three hours earlier, the tentacled alien passengers huddled together protectively. They wrapped their tentacles tight around one another, and the screams they'd let out when Gabriel was killed slowly fell away to a murmur. They weren't going to be any help, thought Martha. She was all there was.

She stepped forward. 'Who are you?' she asked the badgers.

'Name's Dashiel,' said the badger who'd killed Gabriel. He waved a bony, hairy paw at his counterparts. 'That's Jocelyn, and that's Archibald.' Martha couldn't suppress a smile. 'What?' Dashiel growled.

'Nothing,' said Martha. 'Was it middle-class parents?'

'We don't have parents!' said Archibald, the other male badger from behind her. He seemed a lot younger than the other two. 'We was grown in a lab.'

'Archibald,' Dashiel chided. 'She dun't need to know

that.' He didn't sound, thought Martha, like someone doing an impression of a pirate – all "me hearties" and "shiver me timbers". They were like the teenagers loitering outside the Co-op in the evening, because they had nowhere better to go. Yet the guns were real, and the passengers were terrified. And they'd just disintegrated Gabriel for no reason. She had to take this seriously.

'What do you want?' she said.

Dashiel ran forward and suddenly grabbed her throat. His claws were sharp, grazing her skin. His breath stank of something like cat food. The stench brought tears to her eyes.

'You, girlie,' leered Dashiel. 'We wan' you to shut yer mouth.'

Martha nodded, eyes open wide. OK, now she was scared.

'Dash,' said the other pirate; the gruff-sounding woman, Jocelyn. 'We gotta ask 'em questions.'

Dashiel considered and, for a moment, Martha thought he might just kill her anyway. Slowly he released his grip on her throat. She could still feel the pattern of his claws on her skin and wondered how badly she'd bruise.

'Right,' said Dashiel, addressing the whole room. The tentacled aliens squawked with fear, like so many terrified chickens. Martha could remember a time when she too might have been cowed by the sight of strange gun-toting aliens. Now it was just any other day. 'We wanna know where your captain is!' demanded Dashiel.

'We wanna know where your engines is! And we wanna know why none of you tried to fight us!'

The alien passengers cowered, too terrified to respond.

Martha could see Dashiel would think nothing of killing a few of them, if only to prompt an answer. 'We're all just passengers,' she said, trying to keep the terror from her voice. 'We're civilians. We don't know any of that stuff.'

Dashiel considered this. 'Hurr,' he sighed.

'What we gonna do, Dash?' asked Archibald.

'Don't bovver 'im,' Jocelyn warned him. 'You 'ave to show respect.'

Dashiel brooded. 'We gotta wait for the others. Captain Florence will 'ave orders.'

'Will she let us kill 'em?' asked Archibald eagerly.

Dashiel smiled at him, fondly. 'Maybe. If you be'ave.'

They waited. Martha counted to ten, trying to keep her cool. Any minute now the Doctor would stroll in and everything would get sorted. She kept counting – to twenty, to thirty… There was still no Doctor by the time she got to sixty, and she'd been counting more and more slowly. Oh well, she thought. It looked like she'd have to do the sorting.

'So,' she asked Dashiel amiably, 'how many of you are there?'

'A hundred,' said Dashiel.

'More like a thousand!' said Jocelyn. 'We're like a swarm or an army.'

'Yeah,' agreed Archibald. 'A thousand's bigger than a hundred, is'nit?'

'A bit bigger, yes,' said Martha. 'So where are the other nine-hundred-and-ninety-seven of you?'

'They should be here, Dash,' said Jocelyn. Martha realised Jocelyn had pink lipstick around her hairy mouth. It was one of those pastel shades that Martha didn't suit. It looked quite good on the badger.

'They should be here,' admitted Dashiel. His shiny black nose twitched with irritation.

'Did they get lost?' asked Archibald.

'How'd they get lost, Archie?' said Jocelyn, not unkindly.

'Dunno,' said Archie. He shrugged. 'I get lost sometimes.'

Dashiel raised one arm and spoke into the computer set into his wrist. 'Captain Florence,' he said. 'We need orders.' The response was a hiss of static. Dashiel tried again, sending the same message over and over and getting no reply. Martha could see him getting more and more worried. And she didn't like what that might mean for the prisoners.

'They ain't there,' he said eventually, with terrifying calm.

'So what we gonna do?' asked Archibald, almost on his tip-toes with excitement.

'We're gonna do what the captain told us,' said Dashiel. 'We're gonna find what we came for. We're gonna nick it and then we're gonna wreck the whole ship.'

'Yeah!' agreed Archibald.

'You're gonna stay here, Archie,' Dashiel told him. 'Me and Joss are gonna go take a look-see.'

'Awww!' said Archibald.

'Now, now,' Joss told him gently. 'This way you guard the prisoners. And kill 'em if they make trouble.'

'I s'pose,' said Archibald sulkily.

'Good lad.'

Archibald took Dashiel's position, guarding the only door into the cocktail lounge. Martha noticed how he stood up straighter, looked more mature, given this responsibility. He gave the impression that he *wanted* the prisoners to try something, so he could teach them a lesson.

'Won't be long,' said Dashiel as he and Jocelyn set off. 'Have fun.'

The alien passengers kept quiet, huddled together in front of the bay window. Martha heard them gasp as she made her way slowly to the bar. It was all she could think of to help them. The serving robot stepped neatly up to serve her – he must have been programmed to fetch drinks whatever the circumstances. Martha rather liked that.

'Hydrogen hydroxide on the rocks,' she told him loudly. 'And don't be stingy with it.' The robot quickly fetched her the glass of water and ice cubes while she perched herself on a barstool. In the long mirror behind the bar, she could see Archibald watching her closely. He didn't know quite what to do. She raised an eyebrow at him, like she'd do with any staring bloke in a pub. And just like any staring bloke, Archibald looked quickly away.

Gotcha, thought Martha.

She didn't turn round; she addressed his reflection, left him talking to her back. 'So,' she said in her best sexy voice. 'You're learning to be a pirate.'

She saw him screw up his hairy face. 'I'm not learnin' nuffin',' he said. 'I *am* a pirate.'

'Course you are,' she said. 'Don't let anyone tell you otherwise.'

She watched him seething. 'Captain Florence,' he said at last, 'says we're not pirates anyhow. Says we're *venture capitalists.*'

'Well fancy,' said Martha. She took a slow sip of water, making him wait. Her sister had taught her the knack of it – Tish lived to torture boys. 'So, venture capitalist like you,' she went on. 'Must spend a lot of time in places like this. Sipping cocktails. Doing deals.'

'Yeah,' said Archibald. He was, she knew, lying through his prominent teeth. 'All'a time.'

'Thought so,' she said. 'You'll have a drink, then?'

Archibald bristled. 'What?' he said.

'Just a drink. Nothing heavy.' As she looked down at her glass of water again she winked at him. Just at the last minute, so he might think he'd imagined it. When she glanced up again, she could see him blushing underneath his coarse fur.

'I, uh, yeah,' he said. 'But Dash wouldn't like it.'

'Dashiel can have a drink when he gets back,' she said. 'It's not like he's missing out. The bar's free anyway. And guarding prisoners… That's thirsty work.'

Archibald coughed, clearing the dryness in his throat. He leant back to look through the door into the ballroom, to see if his colleagues were anywhere nearby. Then he waved his gun at the alien prisoners cowering in front of the bay window. The aliens squealed in terror – exactly the response he wanted. As Archibald made his way slowly to the bar, shoulders back, walking tall, Martha could see him playing it cool. He leant against the bar beside her, the perfect position to talk to her and at the same time watch the prisoners. She smiled demurely at him and he grinned back. His breath was hot and stinky, his fur bristly like an old toothbrush.

'Yes, sir?' said the robot barman. Archibald's eyes showed a moment of panic.

'What should I 'ave?' he asked Martha.

She looked him up and down, appraising him. 'Big strong bloke like you?' she said. 'I bet you can handle anything.'

'Yeah,' he agreed. 'I bet that too.'

Martha nodded at the robot. 'Do your worst,' she told it. The robot began to mix various brightly coloured liquids into a glass. Archibald watched in horror as the final concoction was presented to him. The amber liquid let off a haze of steam.

Martha raised her glass of water, chinked it against his drink. 'Down the hatch,' she said, and knocked back her water in one go.

'Yeah,' said Archibald, 'OK.' And he knocked the amber liquid back –

– and then spat it all over the bar. He bent over double, coughing like a well-seasoned smoker. Martha would have made a move to relieve him of his gun but she could see how tight he kept his grip on it. She decided not to risk it.

The robot barman quickly set to work with a towel, tidying up the mess. Archibald wiped the syrupy drool from his chin with the back of his hairy paw. He shrugged at Martha.

'Heh,' he said. 'Didn't really like it.'

'No?' said Martha, as if she'd not seen anything. 'Oh well.'

He stuck his tongue out. 'An' now I got this horrid taste,' he said.

'Oh dear,' said Martha. 'Maybe you should try something else.'

Archibald's glared at the robot barman, his dark eyes narrowing to slits. 'Nah,' he said. 'I'm bored wiv drinking.'

'Yeah,' said Martha, keen to keep him on her side. 'It is a bit boring. What about something to eat?'

Archibald nodded eagerly. 'Yeah,' he said. 'I'm not bored of eating.'

He followed her to the end of the bar and the silver trays loaded with nibbles. The tentacled aliens hurried out of their way, careful to huddle at the other end of the bay window and not to get too close to the door out into the ballroom. Archibald glared at them, reminding them who was boss, then turned back to the waiting nibbles. There were sausage rolls and posh things wrapped in bacon. Martha watched his eyes light up.

'I never ate this stuff before,' he told her. With great care he reached out for the tray of cheese and pineapple on sticks. He took one and scrutinised it closely, like a jeweller examining a diamond.

'You don't eat the stick,' Martha whispered.

Archibald nodded at this sage advice. 'Right,' he said, but made no move to eat it.

Martha helped herself to her own cheese and pineapple stick and showed him how to eat it. She placed the stick back on the tray, in the little silver box provided. Archibald watched her attentively, as if she'd just performed great magic.

'Right,' he said, and did his best to copy the easy way she'd eaten hers. He nibbled warily at first, but after the first taste of pineapple there was no stopping him. When he'd finished, he dropped the clean stick into the silver box and then grinned a happy, badger grin.

'Good?' she asked.

'S'OK,' said Archibald.

'You could always make sure. Have another one.'

Archibald's eyes opened wide at the thought of this. He waited for a moment in case she changed her mind, then helped himself to another cheese and pineapple stick. Martha laughed to see him so delighted.

'You've really never had food like this before?' she asked as she watched him take two cheese and pineapple sticks at once.

'Nah,' he said between mouthfuls. 'We get food packs. 'Ave to share 'em. They're OK. If they get recycled right.'

Martha didn't understand. 'Recycled from what?'

Archibald wrinkled his shiny black nose. 'What else?' he said gruffly. 'The toilets.'

Martha could see that yes, perhaps cheese and pineapple on sticks were something of a luxury. She felt her heart going out to him, growing up on a spaceship with the other badger pirates, never going to school or getting his daily five fruit and veg. It would be a dull, brutal, compartmentalised life, and he'd not even been born. Instead, he and his colleagues had been grown in a lab, slaves made to follow orders just like the mouthless men she'd met in the engine room. Despite his slavering jaws working on yet another cheese and pineapple stick, despite his gun, despite everything, she wanted to give him a hug.

But that wouldn't do any good. Any minute now Dashiel and Jocelyn would come back and, whatever they'd found, the prisoners would be in danger. So she hadn't been able to get Archibald drunk. But she had another idea, one that would make him see his prisoners as people and make it harder for him to shoot them.

As he reached for yet another cheese and pineapple stick, she slapped the back of his paw.

'Ow,' he said.

'Where are your manners?' she said.

Archibald considered. 'Think I lost 'em,' he said. 'Sorry.'

'Yeah,' said Martha, acting cross like her mum. 'But there are other people here, aren't there? What about them?'

Archibald looked over at the tentacled aliens, still cowering in fright. 'They don't like this stuff,' he said. 'They're bored of it.'

'Are they really?' said Martha, folding her arms. 'Why don't you offer them the tray and see how bored they are?'

Archibald muttered something under his breath but did as he was told, picking up the tray of remaining cheese and pineapple sticks with one paw and stalking over to his prisoners. In his other paw he held his gun, also pointed at the prisoners.

'Here,' he said to the first prisoner, the orange lady Martha had spoken to earlier. With the gun pointed right at her, Mrs Wingsworth didn't dare to refuse. A long tentacle looped up and round and delicately took hold of a stick. With everyone watching her, she took a tiny, ladylike bite of cheese and fluttered her eyes in false delight.

'Why, dear,' she told Archibald quietly, eager to please him. 'That is simply a delight!'

Archibald grinned at her. 'Yeah,' he said, pleased with himself. He glanced back at Martha, still stood at the bar. She nodded encouragingly at him and he moved into the throng of tentacled aliens, who took the proffered food from him more and more eagerly. Archibald seemed overawed by the attention, grinning at everyone for all he brandished a gun. Soon there was a hubbub of comfortable chatter and even a bit of laughing.

'That was good,' said Martha as Archibald returned to her with the empty tray. He placed it carefully beside the other trays of food and helped himself to a sausage roll.

'Yeah,' he said, about to say something further. But he'd bitten into the sausage roll and his eyes widened in amazement at this incredible new flavour.

'Wait till you try the scotch eggs,' Martha told him.

While Archibald tried each of the different nibbles on offer, Mrs Wingsworth came over to join them. 'I wonder,' she said, 'if there are any more of those delightful cheese and pineapple ones.'

'Sorry,' said Martha. 'All gone.'

But Archibald then offered Mrs Wingsworth a whole tray of them. Mrs Wingsworth let out a high, girlish giggle as she deftly took one. 'Oh, you are an angel,' she said.

'Yeah,' agreed Archibald.

'Hang on,' said Martha, pointing at the tray laden with cheese and pineapple on sticks. 'Where did that come from?'

'It was 'ere,' said Archibald, indicating the end of the bar where all the trays of nibbles waited. 'Did I do it wrong?'

'But there was only one tray of these things,' said

Martha. 'And we finished it.'

'Yeah,' agreed Archibald.

Martha looked again at the bar. 'Where's the empty tray?' she said. 'The one you just put down?'

Archibald scrutinised the bar himself but could see no empty tray. He shrugged, then seemed to notice the full tray he was still holding. He lifted it up for Martha to see. 'Here,' he said.

Martha boggled. The robot barman was at the far end of the bar, and she was *sure* she would have seen him if he'd come down this end to restock the nibbles. Maybe they had special trays in the future, she thought, which just filled up again the moment the food ran out. Maybe they used the same technology as the teleporter thing she and the Doctor had seen down in the engine rooms.

'I never had stuff like this before,' Archibald told Mrs Wingsworth.

But no, thought Martha, something was wrong. She could feel it. After all these months travelling with the Doctor, she'd developed a sort of sixth sense for things like this.

Her thoughts were cut short by Mrs Wingsworth's mocking laughter. 'Well of course you haven't had food like this before, dear,' she told Archibald. 'You weren't born to this sort of lifestyle, were you?' She probably didn't mean to sound so unkind, thought Martha, but it was hardly wise to antagonise the badger with the gun.

'Look,' she said, trying to intercede.

'I wasn't born,' said Archibald proudly. 'I got grown

in a test tube.'

'Precisely, dear, precisely,' said Mrs Wingsworth. 'And you were grown with a purpose in mind. We need someone to do the grubby jobs, don't we?'

'Huh?' said Archibald.

'What Mrs Wingsworth means—' began Martha.

'She means we're dirty,' said Dashiel as he and Jocelyn marched back into the cocktail lounge. 'And she's right, ain't she? We are dirty. We *fight* dirty. An' we don't care when we kill our prisoners.'

Mrs Wingsworth seemed poised to protest but thought better of it. Which was just as well, thought Martha, as the pirates were in an even worse mood than before. Judging by the surly looks on their faces they hadn't found what they were after.

'What's been 'appenin', Archie?' Dashiel demanded.

Archibald carefully put the tray of cheese and pineapple sticks back down on the bar and headed over to his colleagues. His body sagged as he went over, Martha noticed. When it had just been him, he looked taller, tougher, more in control. When the others badgers were around, though, he became like a sulky teenager.

'I was askin' 'em questions,' he told Dashiel.

'Find anythin' out?' Dashiel asked him.

'Nah,' said Archibald. 'They're pretty stupid.'

Martha couldn't stop Mrs Wingsworth. 'Well really!' she huffed, more than a little too loudly.

'You got summin' to say, 'ave you?' growled Dashiel, jabbing his gun towards her.

Mrs Wingsworth trembled where she stood. 'No,' she squeaked.

Martha reached out her hand and took hold of Mrs Wingsworth's tentacle. There was little she could do if the badgers turned on any of the prisoners, but Mrs Wingsworth seemed grateful for the gesture and her trembling began to ease.

'Don't annoy them,' Martha whispered.

'I don't mean to, dear,' Mrs Wingsworth whispered back. 'But, you know, I mean *really*...'

The three badger pirates conferred by the door back into the ballroom. Martha edged forward to better hear what they were saying, but Mrs Wingsworth held her back.

'Don't, dear!' she whispered. 'They'll kill you.' And Martha didn't need to get any nearer; Dashiel was so angry he didn't bother to keep his voice down.

'We found the bridge,' he growled, 'but couldn't get in there.'

'An' we couldn't find the engines,' said Jocelyn.

'It's that door with the stuff,' Dashiel told her. 'I bet you.'

'Could be,' said Jocelyn. 'But you know what Captain Florence'd say. You can't *prove it*, can you?'

'An' what about the others?' asked Archibald.

Dashiel glanced over at Martha and the tentacled aliens before he said anything further. He whispered, but Martha didn't need to hear the words. To want to keep it secret could mean only one thing: these three badgers were all there were. And Martha could deal with three badger-faced pirates.

'There's food here if you want it,' she said, gathering up the tray of cheese and pineapple on sticks and taking it over to them. Again the tray had replenished itself; despite what Archibald had taken just a moment ago, the tray was full again.

'What's this?' asked Jocelyn warily.

'Oh, yeah,' said Archibald. 'You should try these.' He showed his colleagues how to eat the cheese and pineapple and what to do with the sticks. Dashiel and Jocelyn followed his example, and like him their eyes widened with amazement.

'That's amazing!' said Dashiel. 'That's like…' He trailed off, unable to think of words to describe what it tasted like.

'It's *nice*!' agreed Jocelyn, wowed by the very idea that food could taste good.

'You,' said Dashiel, prodding Martha with his paw. 'What's this stuff called?'

Before Martha could answer she heard a tutting behind her. She didn't need to guess who that was.

'You,' said Dashiel. 'Come 'ere.'

Martha watched in horror as Mrs Wingsworth came forward. Her tentacles trembled with fear but Martha saw her struggling not to show that she was scared.

'I really didn't mean anything by it,' said Mrs Wingsworth, talking quickly. 'But really, dears, it *is* funny. I mean, imagine! You've never even *seen* a canapé.'

'Canner-peas,' growled Dashiel, still holding a half-eaten cheese and pineapple stick. 'That's what they're called?'

'Yeah,' said Martha, trying to calm the situation. 'That's a posh name for finger food. I call them "nibbles".' It was like any family party, with her having to be the peacemaker. Except when her parents argued, they weren't also wielding guns.

'Nibbles,' said Dashiel slowly. 'Cos you nibble on 'em. Yeah.' He seemed quite taken with the word, and finished the cheese and pineapple stick as he considered. Martha stepped forward, proffering the tray so he could put the stick into the little silver box. She didn't withdraw, waiting in front of him until he took another cheese and pineapple stick from her tray. Anything to keep his mind off the gun in his other hand.

'We've also got sausage rolls and scotch eggs,' she told him, 'and those things like baby pizzas.'

'Cor,' said Dashiel and Jocelyn together.

'"Things like baby pizzas"!' said Mrs Wingsworth, aghast.

'What *now*?!' shouted Dashiel, storming over to her. Mrs Wingsworth threw her tentacles up in front of her wide and orange face. The other tentacled aliens quickly withdrew to the far side of the room, leaving Mrs Wingsworth on her own with Dashiel.

'She didn't mean it!' said Martha quickly. She wasn't sure what she could do to stop him, especially with the tray of cheese and pineapple sticks in her hands.

'You shut up,' Dashiel snapped at her. 'Now,' he said to Mrs Wingsworth, prodding her egg-shaped body with his gun, 'you tell me. *What?*'

Mrs Wingsworth seemed to consider her predicament and conclude she had nothing to lose. She visibly relaxed, meeting Dashiel's gaze and holding it.

'I know you can't help it, dear,' she said. 'But you three are just an absolute shambles. Coming aboard like this, all threats and violence. And you don't even know what you're eating! My boys could tell you what made the best blinis – that is what they're called, young woman – before they were fully hatched!'

Dashiel seemed transfixed by the performance. He knew he was being insulted, Martha could see, but he didn't quite understand how. The cheese and pineapple sticks were a brief taste of a life he and his colleagues had never even known. And for all this tentacled alien prisoner taunted him, the insult also gave a tantalising glimpse of a life where you could take this luscious stuff for granted. A life where food had different names.

Martha glanced over at Jocelyn and Archibald. They too were watching avidly, hanging on what Mrs Wingsworth had to say. It was just possible, she thought, that the tentacled alien had made them rethink their pirate ways.

'Yeah,' murmured Jocelyn.

'Yeah,' agreed Archibald hungrily. 'Go on, do it, Dash.'

And Martha suddenly saw that she had got it wrong.

They weren't hungry at the thought of Mrs Wingsworth's world of canapés. They were excited because she'd just given them an excuse to kill her.

'Please,' said Martha, taking the tray of cheese and pineapple sticks with her as she went over to Dashiel.

'I said *shut up!*' he snapped at her, his eyes never leaving Mrs Wingsworth.

Mrs Wingsworth did not look away from him. 'It's all right, dear,' she told Martha. 'I'd rather get it over with now than spend any more time with this *riff-raff*.' She smiled with satisfaction, like somehow she'd just won a board game.

Dashiel took a step back from her and raised his gun.

'No!' cried Martha, dropping the tray to one side as she ran forward. Dashiel swiped her away with one paw, sending her sprawling across the floor, on top of the spilt cheese and pineapple sticks. Stunned, she looked up in time to see Dashiel pulling the trigger.

Mrs Wingsworth didn't scream. She stood tall and sure and haughty as the pink light dazzled round her. Martha watched appalled until there was nothing of Mrs Wingsworth left to see.

SIX

More than three hours later, the Doctor stood in the same cocktail lounge watching the space where until a moment before Mrs Wingsworth had stood. The air was rich with a stink of roasted lemons, and wisps of ash floated from the ceiling, but only the Doctor seemed in any way bothered about what had just taken place.

'You disintegrated her!' he said, appalled.

'Yeah,' said Dash. 'S'only language these lot unnerstand.'

The Doctor blinked at him. 'You disintegrated her!' he said again.

Dashiel grinned. 'You catch on quick,' he said.

The other Balumin prisoners huddled by the bay window, though not from fear, the Doctor noticed. They really didn't seem to give a stuff that Mrs Wingsworth had just been killed and that it might be any one of them next. He ran a hand through his thick hair, not caring that it probably made it all stick up oddly.

'Right,' he said, addressing the badger pirates. 'Well maybe before anyone else gets hurt we can discuss what it is you lot want. From us, from the *Brilliant*, from life in general if you like.' He grinned at them.

Dash regarded him coolly. 'We gotta mission,' he said.

'That's good,' said the Doctor. 'Something to work towards. I like that.'

Dash nodded but said nothing further. The Doctor could see he was going to need some prompting.

'Your mission wouldn't be to pinch the *Brilliant*'s experimental drive, would it?' he said. The badgers stared at him.

'Yeah,' said Archie.

'No,' said Dash at the same time. He glared at Archie, then said to the Doctor, 'It might be.'

'Figured,' said the Doctor. 'It's what I'd be after, if I was a pirate.'

Dash leered at him. 'We ain't pirates,' he said. 'We're entrepreneurs.'

'Oh right,' said the Doctor. 'Sorry, I always get those two the wrong way round. Pirates are the ones with the suits and pink shirts, aren't they? Anyway. I'm thirsty. Aren't you lot thirsty, what with all the entrepreneur-ing? Is there anywhere round here we can get a drink?' He looked all round him quickly and then made out like he'd only just seen the long bar that stretched down one side of the cocktail lounge. 'Ooh!' he said, making his way over to inspect the menu the machine barman offered him. 'A bar! Brilliant! Watchoo all having?'

A long mirror hung behind the bar. In the reflection, the Doctor could see the badgers watching him uncertainly. He hoped to wrong-foot them, keep their attention on him, stop them killing any more of the Balumin prisoners. 'Come on,' he said when the badgers made no move to name the drinks they wanted. 'It's my round. I'm gonna have a blue one.' He pointed to the branka juice on the menu. 'One of those, please,' he asked the barman.

The machine barman smoothly retrieved a branka fruit from a bowl, extended a shiny blade from its skinny arm and in a blur of quick, precise activity chopped the fruit into tiny pieces. 'You wanna watch this guy at work,' the Doctor told the badgers. 'It's like an art or something.'

Archie came over to join him at the bar, but rather than choosing a drink he prodded the Doctor in the arm with one of his long and jagged claws.

'Ow,' said the Doctor.

'We're *bored* of cocktails,' said Archie, making it sound like a threat. Perhaps, thought the Doctor, they weren't allowed to drink while they were out rampaging. These things had to have a certain discipline, didn't they?

'That's a point,' he said. 'I think I'm bored with them too. Hold the juice, barman.' The machine had long since stopped chopping and now stood perfectly still, poised with the glass of thick, blue liquid in its metal hand. It took the Doctor's command entirely literally, and held on to the glass until someone told it otherwise. Machines, thought the Doctor, could be dim like that.

He turned to Archie. 'So,' he said breezily. 'What else is there that isn't cocktails?'

Archie grinned at him. 'We got canapés,' he said. Sure enough, trays full of elegant finger food were laid out at the other end of the bar, by the bay window.

'Cor,' said the Doctor, 'they do look exciting, don't they?' He leant closer in to Archie for a conspiratorial whisper. 'Which ones do you recommend?'

Archie considered. 'The ones with the sticks,' he said. 'They're good.'

The Doctor scratched at his chin as he nodded, considering this advice. He made his way slowly to the other end of the bar and, looking up to make sure Archie was still watching, took one of the cheese and pineapple sticks. He then tried to put the whole thing in his mouth.

Alarmed, Archie hurried over. 'You don't eat the sticks!' he said.

The Doctor removed the cheese and pineapple stick from his mouth and scrutinised it closely, as if trying to make sense of its workings. If in doubt, he thought, always play it stupid. It put people – and, he hoped, badger-faced pirates – at their ease.

'Like this,' said Archie, grabbing his own cheese and pineapple stick. The Doctor watched him as he nimbly ate the pineapple and then the cheese from around the stick, and then did his best to copy the procedure –

careful to make it look like he'd never done this before. If he could put Archie at his ease, make him drop his guard… One chunk of pineapple escaped him, slipped down his chin and slapped into the carpet between his trainers.

'Oops,' said the Doctor. 'It's pretty tricky, this.'

'Yeah,' said Archie, helping himself to another cheese and pineapple stick.

'Archie!' growled Dash, still by the door back into the ballroom, still brandishing his heavy gun. 'I said no more. You'll be sick.'

'I don't feel sick,' said Archie.

'Do what Dash says,' growled Joss. The Doctor watched Archie put his cheese and pineapple stick back on the tray behind them. He turned back to say something to Dash, and then a sudden thought struck him. He looked back at the tray, on which the cheese and pineapple sticks were crowded. There was no space to fit any more on the tray. There was no empty space from the two cheese and pineapple sticks he and Archie had eaten.

He glanced up at the robot barman, still at the other end of the bar, still holding the glass of branka juice until someone told it not to. It had not nipped over to top up the cheese and pineapple sticks. The Doctor looked again at the tray and then around it at the fittings on the bar. No, he could discern no transmat technologies or any other clever doodads which might automatically replenish the tray.

'Good, innit?' said Archie.

'Very good,' said the Doctor. 'And no matter what you eat, the food just keeps coming?'

'Yeah,' said Archie. 'An' we eat a lot.'

'It's true, dear,' said Mrs Wingsworth as she walked into the cocktail lounge, brushing past Dash and Joss. 'They've been gorging themselves for hours!'

'You,' snarled Dash, 'get wiv the others.'

'Yes, dear,' said Mrs Wingsworth in a mocking, sing-song voice. Dash and Joss kept their guns trained on her, but didn't seem surprised to see her. Neither, noted the Doctor, did the other Balumin prisoners.

'Er,' said the Doctor. 'I don't mean to be rude, but didn't I see you die?'

'Oh *that*,' said Mrs Wingsworth, batting a tentacle at him like his question were some irksome insect.

'It's annoying,' growled Archie.

'Yes, it is a bit of a nuisance, isn't it?' agreed Mrs Wingsworth. 'Every time they shoot one of us down, we just wake up in our berths. It's an outrage, you know.'

'I can imagine,' said the Doctor, baffled.

'They're really not what we were promised,' Mrs Wingsworth continued. 'We're meant to be first class. And they've given us tiny spaces!' She was talking about the berths, the Doctor realised, not about having been killed.

'She's gotta point,' said Archie. 'I 'ave more room to myself on my ship!'

'Well, it's part of the experience,' said the Doctor.

'Bit of discomfort to sharpen the senses. I'm sorry, it's Mrs Wingsworth isn't it? I didn't know the Balumin had regenerative powers like that.'

'No?' asked Mrs Wingsworth. 'Well, they do say schools are dumbing down, don't they?'

'S'a bit of a swizz, you ask me,' said Archie. 'You kill someone, they should stay killed.'

'Yeah,' agreed Dash, from over by the door.

'That's more a reason why you *shouldn't* kill anyone,' chided the Doctor. 'Isn't it?'

'I'd like to know what my Uncle Cecil would have made of it,' said Mrs Wingsworth airily. 'He was a famous consultant, you know. Treated the Yemayan Ambassador, Mr Sutton. Was quite something at the time. And he was very interested in this sort of thing. I think he even wrote about it.'

'I'll have to look that up,' said the Doctor. 'When I've a spare moment. Though I can probably guess what he concluded.' He looked Mrs Wingsworth up and down quickly, and again she batted him away with a tentacle. 'Speed of recovery like that, you've probably got a nifty gift for remyelinating nerve fibres at a rate of knots. Obvious really, isn't it?'

'If you say so, dear,' said Mrs Wingsworth.

'You disintegrate them,' said Archibald slowly. 'And they get better.'

The Doctor grinned. 'That's the gist of it, yeah. Glad you're keeping up. Must be a characteristic of the Balumin. But I hadn't heard of it before.'

'Is there ways to kill them?' asked Joss. 'So they don't come back?'

'No idea,' said the Doctor. 'And I'm not sure I want to find out.'

'You're boring,' said Archie.

'Well maybe I am. But at least I don't go round killing people for no very good reason.'

'They're quite indescribably brutish,' agreed Mrs Wingsworth. 'No manners whatsoever!'

'I'm warning you,' began Dash, angrily.

'Oh, what are you possibly going to threaten me with next, dear?' asked Mrs Wingsworth lightly. 'You stand there with your great big gun and yet we both know you're completely impotent.'

'Hang on, hang on,' said the Doctor, quickly putting himself between Dash and Mrs Wingsworth before things turned ugly again. 'Mrs Wingsworth, with all due respect, that's not really helping. And Dash, you know it does no good to kill her, so let's not waste everyone's time.'

Dash and the other two badgers glowered at him, but since they did not say anything it looked like they took his point. Mrs Wingsworth clearly wasn't used to being talked to like that either, but she too yielded with wounded grace.

'Good,' said the Doctor. 'Now, we're in a bit of a pickle, aren't we?'

He would have elaborated further, got the pirates and the prisoners working together to work out what had happened to the *Brilliant*. But Archie interrupted, muttering something gruffly under his breath.

The Doctor turned to him wearily. 'What is it?' he asked.

'Nothing,' said Archie.

'No, it was definitely something,' said the Doctor. 'Spit it out so everyone can hear.'

Archie glanced at his badger comrades, but they weren't going to help him with this. 'Well,' he told the Doctor, in an embarrassed tone. 'It was jus' different with that girl.'

'That girl?' said Doctor. He beamed. 'Archie, you've met my friend Martha!'

'Yeah,' said Archie proudly. 'She was good.'

'Oh,' said the Doctor. 'She's better than good.'

'Yeah,' said Archie. 'When we killed her she knew to stay dead.'

More than three hours earlier, Martha had stood in the same cocktail lounge watching the space where until a moment before Mrs Wingsworth had stood. The air was rich with a stink of roasted lemons, and wisps of ash floated from the ceiling. Martha felt sick to her stomach.

'That was murder!' she said coldly.

'Yeah!' said Archibald. But he saw the horror in her eyes and looked quickly away.

'She 'ad it coming,' said Dashiel, gruffly. 'Anyone else wanna be difficult?'

The alien prisoners quavered with fright, none daring to respond. Dashiel seemed delighted. He growled at them, he jabbed his gun at them, each time getting them to scream.

'Ha!' he said. 'This is good!'

'Let me kill one, Dash,' said Jocelyn, coming to his side. 'Go on! Archie got to kill one.'

'You can't!' said Martha.

'I didn't *mean* to kill one,' said Archibald quietly, still looking guilty.

'Yeah you did!' said Jocelyn. 'That was good!'

'Yeah,' agreed Archibald, though he still didn't seem convinced. Martha saw how he kept glancing at her, keen for her approval.

'All right,' said Dashiel. 'Which one you wanna kill?'

The aliens shrieked with terror as Jocelyn looked them over. She decided on a pale blue male, who wore several watches on his left tentacle.

'Please,' said Martha. 'We'll cooperate.'

'There's nothing *to* operate,' said Dashiel, seeming pleased with himself at using such a long word. 'Get on with it, Joss.'

Jocelyn grinned as she pulled the trigger and the pale blue alien vanished in brilliant pink light. Martha didn't think – she just ran forward and grabbed the gun from Jocelyn's paws. Startled, Jocelyn let go, fell back, and then quickly took cover behind Dashiel. Martha covered them both with Jocelyn's gun.

'What you gonna do?' snarled Dashiel without any

fear. 'There's a hundred of us coming.'

'They're not coming,' said Martha. 'You know you're on your own.' She tried to wield the gun like she knew what she was doing with it, though she really didn't.

'They are!' said Dashiel, but she could see the fear in his eyes. He took a step towards her.

'Don't do it, Dash,' said Archie. He stood to Martha's left, his gun aimed at her. He didn't look any more confident about using it than she felt about using hers.

'I don't want to hurt anybody,' she said, backing away from them. Maybe she could get behind the bar, use it as cover. Or, back to the wall, she could circle round, get over to the door in the far corner of the cocktail lounge.

'No you don't,' Dashiel told her as he took another cautious step nearer. 'Cos you hurt us an' we 'ave to hurt you more.'

'Keep back!' she told him, her voice more shrill than she'd have liked it. 'I mean it!'

Dashiel did as he was told, his gun still on her, Jocelyn still cowering on the far side of him. Archibald kept looking over at them and back at Martha, and he couldn't keep his feet still. They were children, thought Martha. Badger-faced children dressed up as pirates. But their game had gone too far.

'We can talk about this,' she told them. 'Like grown-ups.'

Dashiel considered. 'Yeah,' he said, and slowly lowered his gun.

And behind him Mrs Wingsworth sauntered into the

cocktail lounge, waving a cheery tentacle. 'Hello, dears!' she cooed. Her flesh was dark and patchy, showing long-healed scars. But Martha had seen her completely consumed by the disintegrating pink light.

The badgers turned round to stare at her, just as amazed as Martha.

'It's impolite to gawp at someone,' said Mrs Wingsworth uncomfortably. 'I expected better from you at least, Martha.'

'Sorry,' said Martha. She took a step back, bumped her bum into the bar and stumbled forward. Before she could do anything Archibald had rushed forward and snatched Jocelyn's gun from her hands. Martha tried to snatch it back but Archibald moved quickly out of reach. She looked round, but the only thing to hand was the tray of cheese and pineapple sticks.

'Well,' grinned Dashiel, raising his gun at her.

'Wait!' said Martha, desperate.

'Yeah, wait,' said Archibald loyally.

'Oh, I wouldn't worry about it, dear,' said Mrs Wingsworth. 'It's over very quickly.'

'Shut up!' said Dashiel. 'I'm gonna do this.'

'But I surrender!' said Martha.

'Yeah,' said Archibald.

'You got to kill someone,' Dashiel told him. 'And Joss did that blue one. It's my turn, innit?'

He aimed the gun.

'All this bother,' tutted Mrs Wingsworth.

Martha grabbed the tray behind her, hurled all the

cheese and pineapple on sticks at Dashiel and made a break for the door. But as Dashiel swatted at the descending nibbles, Jocelyn pounced from behind him, wrestling Martha to the ground. Martha fought back, biting and kicking where she could, but Jocelyn was tougher and more vicious. Her hairy face was coarse like an old toothbrush as she pinned Martha to the floor.

'All right!' admitted Martha, winded.

Jocelyn nodded, smiled and clambered off her. Martha, prone on the plush carpet, the empty silver tray face down beside her, looked up into Dashiel's eyes as he stood over her. The gun was pointed in her face. He hesitated, savouring the moment. Martha sat up, leaning on her elbows, refusing to show fear.

'Go on then,' she said bitterly.

'Yeah,' he said.

'Don't!' cried Archibald. But Dashiel had already squeezed the trigger.

And Martha grabbed the empty silver tray and held it between her and the gun. Furious pink light hit the tray so hard she nearly let it go, but, despite the heat searing her fingers, she hung on for dear life. And then the blast of light was over.

She lowered the tray, her hands shaking from the onslaught, her fingers raw with pain.

'Drat,' said Dashiel and raised his gun again. Jocelyn seemed to reach out a paw to stop him, a strange look on her face. He swatted her paw away and Jocelyn lost her balance, toppling over and hitting the floor hard. Steam curled up from her unmoving body.

'Huh?' said Dashiel.

'Your shot, dear,' said Mrs Wingsworth from over by the door. 'It bounced off Martha's shield and hit your friend.' She tutted again. 'It was only a glancing blow, but I think it was enough.'

Martha stared at Jocelyn's dead body, aware now of an acrid, bonfire stink. She looked up at Dashiel. He seemed frozen where he stood. She felt awful for him. She knew she couldn't wait.

As Dashiel fell to his knees beside Jocelyn's body, Martha got quickly to her feet and made a dash for the door. She still had the tray in her raw and throbbing hands.

'Dash,' she heard Archibald say behind her.

'Get after 'er,' said Dashiel quietly.

'Is Joss—'

'Get after 'er!' Dashiel yelled.

Not thinking where she was going or what she had just done, Martha raced through the ballroom towards the staircase. She took the stairs two at a time, but she knew she couldn't outrun Archibald. The pirates were wiry, tough and strong, and she had nowhere to escape to. She ran down the corridor knowing it was useless. The door to the engine room was still blocked with the cold scrambled egg, and there was no sign of the Doctor.

She turned round. Archibald stood at the end of the corridor, cradling his gun. He pointed it at her, then lowered it again.

'Don't like this,' he told her.

'You don't have to do what he tells you,' said Martha.

'They do stuff if I don't,' he said, making his way slowly towards her.

'But you know it isn't right,' said Martha. She glanced back at the doorway of cold scrambled egg, hoping against hope that the Doctor would step through it. When she turned to Archibald again he was stood right up close to her, his cat-food breath hot and stinky in her face.

'Well then,' she said, with the same sexy voice she'd tried on him before.

'Yeah,' said Archibald nervously. He glanced down at her. 'I liked those.'

She looked down. In her hands, the silver tray was laden with cheese and pineapple sticks.

'Take one,' she said.

Archibald grinned at her and reached out. She hit him hard in the face with the tray. He dropped his gun, staggered back and she kicked him with all her might. Archibald fell back but caught her foot and brought her down with him. They scrabbled on the floor, Martha biting and kicking for her life. Archibald didn't fight back, and she knew he was confused. Maybe he didn't fancy her exactly but she'd got something over him. And she'd use that. She'd use that to escape.

She felt a sudden hot pain in her gut and then she could not breathe. Looking down, she saw the dagger

Archibald had thrust into her stomach.

'Ak,' she said to him, all that she could manage.

And she died.

SEVEN

They dared not meet his gaze; not the pirates, not the Balumin prisoners, not even Mrs Wingsworth, who hovered in the doorway. The Doctor stood, tall and still in the centre of the cocktail lounge, the look in his eyes holding them transfixed and terrified.

'I want to see her body,' he said quietly.

The Balumin prisoners murmured with concern but none would dare come forward. Archie looked like he wanted to say something, but Dash got there first. If there was going to be trouble, thought the Doctor, Dash was the one in charge.

'Er,' he said to the Doctor. 'You can't.'

The Doctor turned to look at him. Dash stepped back, involuntarily, then seemed to remember he still had his heavy gun. He raised it a little, though it seemed less to threaten the Doctor than to make Dash himself feel more at ease.

'Can't?' said the Doctor softly. Dash tried to say

something and faltered under the dark brown, staring eyes. He could only shrug and shake his head.

'She's gone, dear,' said Mrs Wingsworth from the other side of the cocktail lounge. She sounded awkward, like she was not used to speaking kindly.

'Gone,' the Doctor repeated as he turned to her. 'I see.'

'It's what happens,' said Mrs Wingsworth, again not quite making it sound as comforting as perhaps she'd hoped.

'Yeah,' agreed Dash, grateful for an ally.

The Doctor nodded. He could think myriad complex thoughts at once, and a small part of his brain acknowledged that the protocols for deaths in space were much like deaths at sea. Martha's body would have been discreetly, respectfully put overboard to minimise any concern from or risk of disease to those remaining. She would be out there, floating in the darkness, calm and cold and lonely.

Another part of his brain already knew that he would find her, however long it took. He could already see the look on Francine's face when he brought her daughter home, could already feel the Jones family's tide of grief and anger. They would blame him for her death – and they would be right to. Once it would never have occurred to him to brave something like that if he could avoid it. But he knew that Martha would have wanted him to take her back to them, and because of that he would face whatever came.

There were just a couple of things here to sort out first.

He shrugged, smiled and tried to convince those watching him that the storm had passed. 'Anyway,' he said. 'Can't stand idly about all day, can we? Gotta find the captain of this starship and have a little word. Get things back on track, make sure you all live happily ever after.' But the pirates and passengers did not seem convinced: the horror and grief must have still showed in his eyes. 'Oh well,' he said, 'please yourselves.'

Yet as he turned to leave the cocktail lounge, Dash stood in his way. He wielded his heavy gun awkwardly, not quite sure where he should be pointing it.

'He'll shoot you, dear,' said Mrs Wingsworth from over by the wall. 'It's rather tiresome.'

'You're our prisoner,' said Dash, as if embarrassed at having to point it out. 'You do what we say.'

The Doctor jutted out his jaw. 'Or what?' he said. 'You really don't want to try my patience, Dash.'

Dash's paws tightened round the trigger of his gun. 'That a threat?' he growled.

The Doctor grinned at him. 'Course not. But look at it this way. I'm the only one who can sort this mess out for you.'

'There ain't a mess,' said Dash. 'And we're the ones in charge,'

'Really?' said the Doctor. 'The three of you?'

'The others'll be 'ere any minute,' said Joss.

'There's going to be more of them?' moaned Mrs

Wingsworth. 'That will be such a nuisance!'

'Yeah,' said Archie.

'That's right,' said Dash, seeming more confident with his comrades beside him.

The Doctor laughed. 'Let's see how much trouble you three are in when they get here.'

'What you mean?' asked Dash.

'Well, look at you,' said the Doctor. 'Oh, I know it's not been all you expected – there's nothing but nibbles to pillage and so on. But you've been here how many hours and what have you achieved? Have you got into the bridge? No. Have you found the engine rooms? No.'

'We killed some people!' said Dash.

'But not very brilliantly,' the Doctor corrected. 'Only Martha's staying dead. So that's what, one whole person, and in how many hours? You think your comrades are gonna be impressed? That's rubbish!'

'It is rather shoddy,' agreed Mrs Wingsworth. She seemed the only one of the Balumin to take any interest. The others busied themselves with important matters like finger food and drinks. The Doctor could see that they had long since learnt that the badger-faced pirates were at worst a mild inconvenience. It was clear the three badgers knew this, too. They itched with frustration.

'It ain't fair,' said Joss. 'These lot don't die when you kill them.'

To make the point, she shot one of the blue Balumin prisoners. As he disappeared in the familiar, vivid pink light, he merely rolled his eyes.

'Oh, that's brilliant,' said the Doctor. 'What did you just prove that I didn't know already?'

'Um,' said Joss. 'I dunno.'

'Well then,' said the Doctor. 'Maybe if you could stop shooting people, I could explain why killing them isn't working.'

'They got powers,' said Dash. 'We know that.'

'Yes,' said the Doctor. 'The Balumin have powers. But even so, no one's completely indestructible. Well, apart from Captain Scarlet. But I don't think he was real.'

'How d'we kill them?' said Dash eagerly. 'You can tell us what to do?'

'Well,' said the Doctor, rubbing at his chin as if considering whether they were worth telling.

'I don't think you should, dear,' advised Mrs Wingsworth. 'They really do have the most frightful manners.'

'Go on,' said Dash. And he screwed his face up as he dredged from his memory a word he had probably never used before. 'Please,' he said.

The Doctor beamed at him. 'All right,' he said. 'I think the problem is with your guns.'

'Huh?' said Dash, cradling his own heavy gun as if the Doctor might steal it off him.

'Yeah,' said the Doctor. 'Pirates like you, you're gonna have guns that can do just about anything. Stands to reason. Your captain isn't going to send you off pillaging with stuff that's not up to standard.'

'She might,' said Joss.

'Shh!' Dash told her.

'So,' said the Doctor, 'if your guns aren't working they must just be on the wrong setting.'

Dash examined the heavy gun in his paws, looking for switches or buttons that he'd not seen before. There didn't appear to be anything. 'How'd we change it?' he asked.

'Ah,' said the Doctor, 'it's a tricky job and you need to be a bit clever. And it helps if you've got one of these.' He extracted the sonic screwdriver from his inside pocket, flipping it into the air and catching it deftly with his other hand.

'What's that?' asked Archie, like any young boy presented with some new gadget.

'Just a screwdriver,' said the Doctor.

'Huh,' said Dash, still wary. 'Maybe.'

'Ah,' said the Doctor. 'You don't trust me. Well, that's OK. We've only just met after all. And I can see that nothing much gets past you.'

'Yeah,' said Dash.

'OK,' said the Doctor. 'Then how about this. I let you have the sonic screwdriver and you can fix your guns yourselves. It should be setting fourteen, and you just give the power cells a quick buzz.'

Dash snatched the sonic screwdriver from him, though his paws were not really suited to such a slim instrument. The Doctor couldn't resist trying to show him which bits to press, but Dash waved him irritably away. 'I can do it,' he growled. 'Not you.'

He jabbed the end of the sonic screwdriver against the power cell of his gun and pressed the narrow button. The screwdriver buzzed and after a second there was a click from deep within the power cell. Dash looked up at the Doctor, who grinned at him encouragingly.

'Very good,' he said. 'You're a natural.'

Dash hurried over to his comrades but would not let them take the sonic screwdriver from him. He pressed it against the power cells of their guns and pressed the button until he heard the click.

'Now,' he said, aiming his own gun at the huddle of Balumin prisoners who were busy chatting with each other at the bar. The Balumin were too busy gossiping and trying different cocktails to pay him and the other pirates any heed.

'You're not going to shoot them!' squealed Mrs Wingsworth from the other side of the cocktail lounge. She had, it seemed, separated herself from the general mêlée.

'Need to test 'em,' said Dash.

'Yeah,' said Joss, also raising her gun. Archie quickly did the same.

'But Doctor!' said Mrs Wingsworth.

The Doctor shrugged, his eyes fixed on the guns. 'We do need to see that it worked,' he said. Mrs Wingsworth hid her face in her tentacles.

Dash, Joss and Archie all fired at once. The Balumin, quite used to being shot already, did not cry out or respond. Only when nothing at all happened – not even a hint of pink light – did they turn round to face the badgers. It took a moment for it to sink in, then they started to laugh.

'What?' growled Dash.

'Oh dear,' said the Doctor brightly. 'Something must have gone wrong!' He reached a long arm out to Dash and plucked the sonic screwdriver from his paw. 'Oh yeah,' he said, holding the slim tube up to the light. 'I can see what I've done. Setting fourteen in a room full of canapés. Should have thought of that. Sorry.'

'What?' asked Dash, though his tone suggested he'd already resigned himself to the inevitable.

'Oh,' said the Doctor. 'It's nothing really, but you just disabled the power cells. The guns won't work any more.'

'You broke them!' growled Dash.

'Oh no,' said the Doctor. 'You did that. I was over here, minding my own business and you—'

Dash charged at him, drawing a dagger from the back of his sleeve as he did so. The Doctor stood his ground, sidestepping only at the last minute. Dash ran headfirst into the great bay window that looked out onto the Ogidi Galaxy. There was a dull and awful thud as he hit the toughened glass, which didn't even waver – he might as well have run headlong into a brick wall. He fell back, his wet black nose squished against his hairy face, and then toppled over, unconscious.

'That was clumsy,' said the Doctor, crouching down beside Dash to examine him. 'You just sleep it off.' When he was sure Dash had done no serious harm to himself, he collected the dagger from where Dash had dropped it, and slipped it into the jacket pocket of his suit.

'You hurt him!' said Joss, covering the Doctor with the gun they both knew could not hurt him.

'I suppose I did,' said the Doctor. 'But not quite as much as he wanted to hurt me. Now, I'm going to the bridge to talk to the captain. Are you going to be stupid enough to try to stop me?'

Joss considered. 'No,' she said. She dropped her useless gun on to the floor and went over to kneel by the unconscious Dash.

'Coming?' said the Doctor to Mrs Wingsworth.

'Me, dear?' she said, amazed. 'Why ever would I?'

'I dunno,' said the Doctor. 'Adventure. Excitement.' He nodded his head at the other Balumin passengers. 'This lot being really boring.' The Balumin prisoners ignored the remark, so he turned on them. 'Don't you ever say anything?' he asked. 'Oi, you cloth-eared lot! I crave the indulgence of an answer!'

The Balumin prisoners seemed to find this rudeness absolutely shocking. 'We do,' said one of the blue ones, his tentacles curling in distaste, 'but only to persons worth speaking to.'

'Oh,' said the Doctor. 'Well you carry on with the complimentary drinks and I'll take my worthless self off out the way and go save all your lives.' They didn't even respond.

'I wouldn't worry, dear,' said Mrs Wingsworth. 'My

great-aunt Amy – she wrote the *High Tea* novels, you know – said our class was often incapable of anything but indulgence. I'm not sure she meant it as a criticism. But yes, I do think I rather fancy a tour of the bridge, since you were so kind as to extend the invitation.'

'Good!' said the Doctor. 'Welcome aboard. I don't suppose it's gonna do much good telling you not to wander off and things?'

'The very idea!' said Mrs Wingsworth, with a light and tinkling laugh.

'Er,' said Archie.

'Yes, Archie?' said the Doctor.

'Er,' said Archie again. 'Can I come? Wanna see stuff.'

'Oh, really!' laughed Mrs Wingsworth. 'You don't think, after everything, that you'll be—'

'As long as you behave,' the Doctor interrupted.

'What's that mean?' said Archie.

'You see!' said Mrs Wingsworth.

'You do as you're told,' the Doctor explained. 'Say please and thank you. Don't try to kill anyone.'

Archie considered. 'Don't see why,' he said gruffly, 'but OK.'

'Good,' said the Doctor, clapping his hands together. 'Well, no time like the present. Allons-y,' and he marched out of the cocktail lounge. Archie and Mrs Wingsworth had to run to catch him up.

At the far end of the ballroom, to the left of the stairs, a small door led off to another narrow passageway. They followed this to a steep flight of metal stairs, the plush wood and carpet of the first-class compartments giving way to simple, whitewashed walls and thick metal.

'It's all very… functional,' Mrs Wingsworth concluded as she made her way upstairs, though she couldn't keep out of her disapproving tone a glimmer of fascination.

They followed the passageway past cramped and uninspiring spaces where the crew might sleep or spend their free time. And then the Doctor stopped abruptly.

'Cor,' he said. 'That's a bit clever.'

A small space capsule, about the size of Smart car, sat in the middle of the deck. The thick, arrow-headed front of the capsule looked a bit like some kind of snow plough, and had clearly ripped its way through the starship's side. The gaping hole in the ship's thick metal wall had been filled with what might have been strawberry jelly but the Doctor recognised as sealant. For a moment he thought of the ship's crew, who must have been sucked out into space as the hole had been gouged. The *Brilliant*'s emergency systems had then filled the gap with sealant, keeping everyone else on board alive.

'I guess that's you,' said the Doctor to Archie.

'Yeah,' said Archie. 'Dash did the driving.'

'You came over in that?' laughed Mrs Wingsworth, appraising the tiny capsule. 'There's surely not room for the three of you!'

'I 'ad to sit on Joss's lap,' Archie explained. He grinned. 'It was good.'

'They'll have hundreds of capsules like this,' said the Doctor. 'They spurt from the mothership in their hundreds, and whoever they're attacking might shoot down a few of them, but some are still going to get through. They're zippy, manoeuvrable… And a bit good really.'

'It all sounds very reckless,' said Mrs Wingsworth, but she seemed quite thrilled by the idea.

'Yeah,' Archie agreed.

The Doctor had climbed behind the steering wheel and was checking over the controls and read-outs. 'I just wondered if there was anything that might tell us what happened to all your comrades,' he said. 'Seems odd only one of you made it aboard.'

'We won the race,' said Archie proudly. 'Get the best spoils that way, Dash says.'

'I see,' said the Doctor. He opened the glove compartment and eight chunky gold earrings fell out on to the floor. 'Sorry,' he said to Archie.

'S'all right,' said Archie. 'They're a bonus.'

'You could wear one in each ear, couldn't you?' said Mrs Wingsworth. 'It would be tidier that way.'

'Nah,' said Archie, 'that's not what they're for.'

'The single loop is an old tradition,' the Doctor explained. 'If Archie here gets himself killed, his comrades can claim his earring as payment for seeing he gets a decent funeral.'

'Yeah,' said Archie. 'It's proper, ain't it?'

'That is rather considerate,' said Mrs Wingsworth. 'In my family, any death is an excuse for yet another squabble over property and jewels. You can't imagine how much of my life I've had to spend negotiating probate. It's a good thing we're such a close family, really; it makes it easier to hand out the subpoenas.'

'What she on about?' Archie asked the Doctor.

'Oh,' said the Doctor. 'Fighting. Over money. Just your sort of thing.'

Archie grinned at Mrs Wingsworth, seeing in her something new, something he understood. 'Good,' he said.

'If Martha was here,' said the Doctor, clambering back out of the small capsule, 'you know what she would say?'

'No,' said Archie, hanging his head.

'Really?' said the Doctor. 'You don't have any idea?'

'She wouldn't like it,' Archie admitted.

'That's right,' said the Doctor. 'And you know what? Just for her, I'm gonna make sure you lot change your ways.' He met Mrs Wingsworth with his terrible gaze. 'All of you,' he said.

'What are you implying, dear?' laughed Mrs Wingsworth, though without the lightness that her words suggested.

'S'OK,' said Archie. 'Was bored of killing them lot anyway. S'no fun when they just come back.'

'Really?' said the Doctor, sternly. 'Killing Martha was much better for you, was it?'

Archie again hung his head. 'No,' he said.

'He was rather upset about it,' Mrs Wingsworth told the Doctor.

'When I first met her,' said the Doctor, 'she was training to be a doctor. She wanted to help people. Wanted to make things better. And she did. Wherever we went, she made things better. And I couldn't have been more proud of her. She was going to do brilliant things.' His smiled faded. 'And you stopped her.'

Archie scratched awkwardly at his ear. 'I never 'ad a friend before,' he said quietly. 'An' she was nice. She let me eat food.'

'Yes,' said the Doctor. 'But it wasn't enough, was it?'

'But,' said Archie. 'I thought… I wanted to give 'er a funeral.'

'He did talk about that,' said Mrs Wingsworth.

'She didn't 'ave an earring, so I took this instead,' said Archie. And he dipped his paw into his spacesuit and extracted the thin chain that he wore round his neck. The innocent-looking key to the TARDIS spun slowly from the chain.

'That's stealing, dear,' said Mrs Wingsworth.

'I'll take it,' said the Doctor. 'I'm going to take Martha home to her family.'

Archie considered, and then removed the chain from round his neck and handed it to the Doctor. 'Can I come too?' he said.

'Of course you can't!' said Mrs Wingsworth.

'Oh,' said Archie sadly.

'Her family wouldn't take it too well,' said the Doctor. 'They're not going to be happy seeing me.'

'And also,' said Mrs Wingsworth, 'there isn't a body.'

'I'll find her,' said the Doctor. 'However long it takes.'

'If you say so, dear,' said Mrs Wingsworth.

'But it's good that you feel bad about it, Archie,' said the Doctor. 'It means there's hope for you yet.'

'Don't like it,' said Archie. 'It's sad. Like Dash, when Joss got killed.'

'What?' said the Doctor.

'Oh,' said Mrs Wingsworth. 'When they chased your friend, Jocelyn got in the way of the shooting. I think it reflected off the tray Martha was holding.'

'An' Dash was sad,' said Archie. 'He was crying.'

'I think it made things clear between them, dear,' said Mrs Wingsworth. 'Said all the things they never dared to.'

'Yeah,' said Archie. 'They're goin' steady now. I saw 'em kissing.'

'Well, that's lovely,' said the Doctor. 'Can't imagine a happier couple and all the things you're meant to say. But you said she died.'

'Yeah,' said Archie. 'Didn't like that.'

'No,' said the Doctor. 'I can see that. But she died. And now she's going out with Dash.'

'Yeah,' said Archie.

'So she just woke up again?' said the Doctor.

'No, she went first,' said Archie. 'Like a transmat. When none of us was looking.'

'It's never when anyone's watching,' said Mrs Wingsworth. 'It's discreet like that.'

'And *then* she woke up,' said the Doctor, hopping from

foot to foot with irritation.

'Yeah,' said Archie. 'Said she woke up here. An' she had her earring in. But Dash took it. So we got two.'

'It was rather comic,' said Mrs Wingsworth. 'They started shooting each other to collect the extra earrings.'

'Yeah,' said Archie. 'It was good.'

'But then,' laughed Mrs Wingsworth, 'they realised that while they're still stuck aboard the *Brilliant* they've nothing to spend the gold on! It really was delicious.'

'Yeah,' said Archie.

The Doctor was staring at them. 'She woke up here?' he said. 'By your capsule?'

'Yeah,' said Archie. 'Me too when I got killed.'

'With me it's in my berth,' said Mrs Wingsworth. 'It's like going back to square one on a board game. Have you played Backgammon?'

But the Doctor didn't answer. He was already away down the passageway, racing back the way they had come.

Racing back to the engine rooms.

EIGHT

The thick metal fire door squealed with protest as it lifted back up into the ceiling. It had only raised a couple of feet when the Doctor rolled underneath it, leapt nimbly up on to his feet and threw his arms round Martha Jones.

'Brilliant,' he said as he hugged her. 'Brilliant brilliant brilliant!'

'Hey,' she said to him, hugging him back but in a strictly friendly way. 'You took your time.'

He withdrew from her, his hands still on her arms like he couldn't quite let her go. His eyes sparkled with delight at her, and again made her insides turn over. 'Well,' he said, making light of it all, 'it took a minute to convince the doors that there wasn't any fire and they could let me through.'

'So why did they come down in the first place, then?' she asked. A thought struck her. 'What have you been up to?'

'It wasn't me!' said the Doctor, as if shocked by the very idea. 'The badgers didn't want anyone else just walking out of the engine rooms. So they set off the emergency things.'

'But there isn't any fire,' said Martha.

'No,' said the Doctor. 'But emergency things aren't meant to ask questions. You want them to react at the first sign of danger and not to think about it. So it's easy to set them off. Getting them to relax afterwards takes a bit of doing.'

'It is a precautionary measure, Mr Doctor,' said a polite, robotic voice from behind Martha.

'Gabriel!' beamed the Doctor at the robot. 'You're in better shape than last time. And you got trapped down here as well?'

'Begging your pardon, Mr Doctor,' said Gabriel, 'I thought it best to remain with Ms Martha in case I could be of assistance.'

'That's very noble of you,' said the Doctor. 'I'm sure Ms Martha appreciates it.'

'Yeah right,' said Martha. 'Kept on offering to fetch me drinks. But could he raise the fire doors?'

'This unit,' said Gabriel, 'may only countermand the door protocols when not to do so would threaten passenger safety.'

'He's been saying that the whole time, too,' said Martha.

'He was only doing his job,' said the Doctor kindly.

'But I've been stuck in here for hours!' said Martha.

'Total duration forty-nine minutes and eighteen seconds,' Gabriel corrected.

'That's about as long as it's been since I got out of the engine rooms,' said the Doctor. 'Give or take a bit. Guess if you'd been brought back any earlier, I could have seen it happen. And that's not how it works.'

'The Starship *Brilliant* is programmed with discretion parameters, Mr Doctor,' said Gabriel. 'We apologise for any delay.'

'It *felt* like hours!' snapped Martha at the robot.

'This unit,' repeated Gabriel, 'may only countermand the door protocols when—'

'What's wrong?' said the Doctor, picking up on Martha's anxiety. 'Martha, what's happened to you?'

'Doctor,' she said gently. 'I *died*. I *really* died.'

'Yeah,' said the Doctor. 'You did.' He grinned at her, that infuriating grin which made you grin back at him. 'But you got better.'

Martha would have said something, but her mouth fell open in horror as she saw who now stood behind the Doctor; Mrs Wingsworth and Archibald.

'What is it?' said the Doctor.

'He…' said Martha, struggling to find the words. 'He killed me. And I think he took the TARDIS key.'

'Yeah,' said Archibald.

'See?' said Martha.

'Yeah,' said the Doctor. 'And then he surrendered it to me, just because I asked him nicely. Here you go.' He dropped the chain with the key on it into her hands.

'Oh,' said Martha as she put the chain around her neck. 'So we're all friends again now, are we?'

Archibald fidgeted nervously.

'You've got something to say to her,' Mrs Wingsworth prompted him. 'Haven't you, dear?'

'Sorry,' said Archibald to Martha. 'Won't do it again.'

'I should hope not!' said Martha. She lifted up her vest top to show him the scar on her belly where the knife had gone in. 'See that?' she said. 'That's what you did to me!'

The Doctor put on his glasses as he bent to examine the scar. 'That's healing nicely,' he said. 'Looks like you've had it for years.'

Archibald also examined the scar. 'Skin's good,' he said. Martha quickly dropped her vest back down.

'Don't go getting any ideas,' she told him.

'No,' said Archibald, guiltily.

'I like having ideas,' said the Doctor. 'Ideas are good. I think I'm having one now. Yes, here it comes.' They waited for him to go on. 'Yes, here we go. Martha, you remember dying.'

Her shoulders sagged at the memory. 'Yeah,' she said quietly.

'And the scar is there to prove it happened, yeah?' he went on.

'I guess so,' said Martha.

'Well, don't you see?' said the Doctor.

'No,' said Martha. She sometimes found his enthusiasm for all things a bit exhausting. 'It's been a long day and you can just tell me.'

'Right,' said the Doctor. 'Now, you died, yeah?'

'Yeah,' said Martha.

'And then you got brought back to life down here. Like being in a board game and having to go back to the start.'

'Yeah,' she said.

'That's what I said,' said Mrs Wingsworth.

'Yes, it's a good analogy, thank you,' said the Doctor. 'But whatever it was that brought you back to life, Martha, whatever made you better… It left you with a scar.'

'Yeah,' said Martha. And then her eyes opened wide with sudden realisation. 'But it didn't need to! Something as powerful as that…'

'It could have made you good as new,' agreed the Doctor.

'But it's not just me,' said Martha. 'It brought back Mrs Wingsworth, too.'

'I don't have any scars,' said Mrs Wingsworth. Then she considered. 'But I did the first time they killed me.'

'We killed them a lot,' explained Archibald. 'An' they never died.'

'It's all very convenient, isn't it?' said the Doctor. 'Like…' He looked to Martha. 'Like what else? Something in the cocktail lounge.'

'The canapés!' she said.

'Canapés are good,' said Archibald.

'So good you ate a whole tray of them,' said Martha.

'And then the moment the tray was empty it was suddenly full again.'

'That's good, too,' agreed Archibald.

'But not when anyone's looking,' said the Doctor. 'It only happens when no one can see how it's done.'

'But *why?*' asked Martha.

'Oh really, dear,' said Mrs Wingsworth. 'The mechanics of these things are so terribly vulgar.'

'Exactly,' said the Doctor. 'It's all part of the well-mannered service. Isn't it, Gabriel?'

They all turned to the robot. His blank, metal head reflected their faces back at them. 'There are protocols, Mr Doctor,' he said.

'You don't really understand it yourself, do you?' said the Doctor, gently.

'I…' began Gabriel. 'The logic is impaired.'

'Yes,' said the Doctor. 'That's the problem, isn't it? You're struggling to make sense of it. The whole starship is.'

'What?' said Martha. 'The starship is thinking?'

'Well, yeah,' said the Doctor. 'Kind of. We can have the philosophy later, but basically it responds to stimuli the best way it can, just like the rest of us. And sometimes we think about it and sometimes we just respond.'

'You mean it's like breathing,' said Martha. 'You can control your breathing consciously, but mostly you don't really think about doing it.'

'That's true of the Balumin, too, dear,' said Mrs Wingsworth. 'Although my cousin Sandy makes a great kerfuffle about how you should *always* control your breathing. She was into all that sort of thing: crystals, coloured smoke…'

'I can hold my breath,' said Archibald proudly. 'For when we go swimming.'

'I think we've established the analogy,' said the Doctor impatiently, always eager to get back to the mystery. 'Now, this ship is going round and round in circles, isn't it? So every day's the same and no one dies for good.'

'It's a time loop,' said Martha. 'Like in that film, *Groundhog Day*.'

'Huh,' said Archibald. 'Groundhogs are bad. They take our stuff.'

'Yes, it is a bit like the film,' said the Doctor. 'Just without all the dancing at the end. And it's not a complete loop. Things don't all go back to the beginning at midnight, they jump back bit by bit. Which suggests the loop is broken somewhere. And we kind of skip over the gap.'

'That's bad, isn't it?' said Martha, seeing the look in his eyes.

'Yes,' he said. 'A closed loop just runs and runs for ever. But with a gap in it, every time it goes round there's something a bit different. You have a scar, you don't have a scar. The badgers come back with new earrings.' He grinned. 'See it didn't try to make another TARDIS key. Probably couldn't understand it. But anyway, all the time it's making things better again, it needs energy. A *lot* of energy.'

'But how?' said Martha. 'What's keeping it all together?'

'There are protocols, Ms Martha,' said Gabriel. But he did not explain any further.

'Yes, there are protocols,' said the Doctor. 'The Starship *Brilliant* doesn't fly through what you think of as reality, Martha. Think of where we are right now as a sort of sea of dreams. And when it's flying normally it needs to get itself back out of that and into the "real" universe. So, as well as the experimental drive itself, it must also be able to twist reality a bit.'

'It *was* all in the brochure, dear,' said Mrs Wingsworth.

'That doesn't sound good,' said Martha. 'You're not supposed to change reality, are you?'

'Well, usually you're all right if you only twist it a bit,' said the Doctor. 'The TARDIS has to be able to warp things about to get in and out of the Vortex. That's your top-end of the clever scale. A ship like this one has just got to make sure the ship holds together and everyone comes out the far end the same shape as when they went in.' He shook his head. 'Though you should see what happens to people when they travel about a lot. Long-term exposure to non-reality, that can be a bit weird.'

'But that's not what's happening here, is it?' said Martha.

'No,' said the Doctor. 'It's working all-out to hold everything together. The *Brilliant* has a rough idea of how things are meant to be, and it tries to keep them like that.

And it's got protocols to look after the passengers and make sure they are safe. So it's restocking the nibbles and bringing you back to life. And all in the most discreet of ways, so you don't quite notice.'

'The service has been exemplary,' agreed Mrs Wingsworth.

'Thank you, Mrs Wingsworth,' said Gabriel. 'I shall pass on your kind words to the captain.'

'The captain,' said the Doctor. 'I should have a word with him, too.'

'I regret to say that the captain cannot meet with passengers at the present time, Mr Doctor,' said Gabriel. 'I would be happy to pass on any message to her.'

'Gabriel,' said the Doctor, 'if I don't speak to the captain myself, the whole ship is in danger. It's only a matter of time before you exhaust the energy available and the *Brilliant* just explodes. And there'll be no more miraculous resurrections then.'

Gabriel considered carefully. 'You believe the passengers are at risk, Mr Doctor?' he said.

'Yes,' said the Doctor.

'Very well,' said Gabriel. 'Please accompany me.'

They followed the robot – left, left again and then right, and up the wide staircase into the dining room. Martha could hear the tentacled aliens yammering away to each other over in the cocktail lounge, oblivious to any danger. A thought struck her.

'Where are Jocelyn and Dashiel?' she asked the Doctor.

'Dash is sleeping,' Archibald told her, eager to be helpful.

'Yeah,' said the Doctor, 'had a nasty bang on his head. Now, we're up here, aren't we?'

He led them off to the side of the dining room and into an area of the ship that clearly wasn't for passengers. There was no wood panelling or plush carpets but whitewashed walls and thick metal. It felt more like the kind of sailing ships Martha had seen in films. They clanged up the steep metal staircase onto the upper level and into a cramped space where the ship's crew appeared to hang out. There were posters on the walls of the tiny sleeping spaces, young and pretty humans waving in 3D.

But Martha had been in the accommodation blocks of hospitals, where the doctors and nurses lived. Her first thought was how tidy these sailors must be. They didn't have books and clothes and DVDs littered all over the floor. She assumed they had to keep their quarters tidy as part of the job. Then she saw the great gash in the ship's metal wall and its cause, the sharp-nosed little space car in the middle of the deck. Everything that hadn't been bolted down had been sucked out into space before the *Brilliant* could seal the hole. She felt a pang of horror at the thought of the sailors who must have died at the same time.

'That's you, is it?' she asked Archibald sourly.

'Yeah,' he replied, but he could not meet her eye. For a moment she felt guilty for being so mean to him. Then she remembered what he'd done to her – the icy pain of the blade as it went through her – and to the other people on board.

'He is trying to be a better badger, dear,' Mrs Wingsworth told her. 'But you have to remember how he's been brought up. I doubt he's been to public school.'

'Went to Eton Nine,' said Archibald. 'S'on an asteroid.'

Mrs Wingsworth quivered with amazement, her long tentacles up to her mouth. 'Really, dear?' she said.

'Yeah,' said Archibald. 'Burnt it down, took the gold.'

'Well that's something of a relief,' said Mrs Wingsworth.

'Is it?' asked Martha. 'I don't see how.'

'Well, dear,' laughed Mrs Wingsworth. 'I was worried for a moment he'd been admitted as a pupil. You know how standards are slipping.'

They followed the Doctor and Gabriel along through the passageway. The small sleeping areas got slightly bigger as they went, and Martha realised they had started in the area for the lowest officers and were now walking up through the ranks. Gabriel opened a heavy door into a chamber full of little rooms, and Martha could see how much better the *Brilliant*'s officers had it. They had proper quarters, with beds and wardrobes and desks.

'Well,' said Mrs Wingsworth. 'I never expected this!'

'Better than what you've got?' asked Martha.

'It's not the privation one minds,' sniffed Mrs

Wingsworth. 'It's the unfairness of it. Why should the captain have such luxury?'

'The captain's recreational area is prescribed by intergalactic law, Mrs Wingsworth,' said Gabriel. 'The regulations require that she does not spend more than thirty consecutive hours on duty, for the safety of the passengers.'

'Oh, I'm sure she's very deserving, dear,' said Mrs Wingsworth. It occurred to Martha she wouldn't normally have called a robot 'dear' – that this was her and the Doctor's influence. 'I just think we should all have the same.'

'It's funny there's no officers about, though, isn't it?' said the Doctor. 'They shouldn't all be on duty at once.'

'They fell off the ship when we came here,' said Archibald. 'Sorry.'

'Even so,' said the Doctor. 'There's no one here.'

'I believe, Mr Doctor,' said Gabriel, 'that many were called to the bridge at the first alarm.'

'Ah,' said the Doctor. 'How many people are there likely to be on the bridge?'

Gabriel considered. 'There are six officers on duty, Mr Doctor, including the captain. There are then twelve reserve officers of which seven are also on the bridge.'

'And why are they there?' asked the Doctor, though Martha suspected he already knew.

'I regret I am not at liberty—' began Gabriel.

'Oh come on,' said the Doctor. 'You know the safety of the passengers is at stake.'

Martha watched Gabriel struggling with his robot conscience. 'They are there in a protective capacity, Mr Doctor,' he said.

'They're there to fight anyone trying to get onto the bridge,' said the Doctor. 'What do you think of that, Mrs Wingsworth?'

'I think it's perfectly understandable, dear,' she said.

'Really?' said the Doctor. 'It doesn't seem very fair to me. Why aren't they out here, protecting the passengers? That's their first responsibility isn't it?'

'Oh,' said Mrs Wingsworth. 'I suppose they did rather leave us in the lurch.'

'We was expectin' to fight,' said Archie. 'But no one 'ere would fight us.'

Martha felt herself growing hot with anger. 'The crew left the passengers to die,' she said. In her mind the crew were already villains anyway: they had to be to employ the poor, mouthless men in the engine room.

'It does look that way,' said the Doctor. 'But let's not judge them until we've heard what they've got to say in response. Here we are.'

They had reached a huge double door at the end of the passageway. Gabriel went forward and, without having to press or say anything, did whatever he had to do. They heard the heavy locks untangling from deep within the doors. Gabriel stepped backwards and the doors swung slowly open at him.

'Oh,' said the Doctor, disappointed. 'Well, yes, I should have thought of that.'

The doorway was blocked by a wall of what looked like scrambled egg. Archibald reached out a hairy paw to prod the strange material. Even when he punched it, the scrambled egg did not yield.

'What are we going to do, dear?' asked Mrs Wingsworth.

'Oh, don't worry,' said Martha. 'The Doctor can get us through. Can't you?'

'Oh yeah,' said the Doctor. 'Nothing simpler. I'm just wondering if I should. It's like with the engine rooms, isn't it? We can get through it easy, we just can't come back out.'

'It's the only way,' Martha told him sternly.

The Doctor gazed at her for a moment. 'Yes,' he said, taking the sonic screwdriver from his inside pocket. 'Yes, I suppose it is.' He clicked the screwdriver to setting twenty-eight and aimed it at the scrambled egg.

Archibald and Mrs Wingsworth watched in wonder. 'What is that?' said Archibald.

'Well, it's just sound waves, really,' said the Doctor, busy at work. 'Vibrations you can aim. This scrambled egg stuff resonates at a certain frequency and that's why it seems solid. If I can change the frequency it all loosens up. And then we just walk through. Simple, really.'

'Yeah,' said Archibald.

'Did you understand that?' asked Martha.

'No,' said Archibald. Martha, despite what he had done to her before, laughed. Archibald grinned at her.

'See, dear?' said Mrs Wingsworth. 'He's rather a

darling once he can stop being such a rascal.'

'Yeah,' said Archibald.

'If you say so,' said Martha. Keen to change the subject, she turned to Gabriel. 'Don't suppose you can get us a drink while we're waiting, can you?'

'Certainly, Ms Martha,' said Gabriel. 'What would you like?'

'I'll have a cup of tea if one's being offered,' said the Doctor, still busy on the door.

'Is tea good?' Archibald asked him.

'Oh,' said the Doctor darkly. 'It's not for everybody. It can be quite dangerous.'

'I'll 'ave a cuppa tea,' Archibald told Gabriel.

'And me,' said Martha. 'Just a bit of milk, no sugar.'

'Certainly, Ms Martha,' said Gabriel. 'And Mrs Wingsworth?'

'A gin and tonic,' said Mrs Wingsworth. 'Well,' she added, seeing how Martha looked at her. 'I *am* on holiday.'

By the time Gabriel returned with the drinks, the Doctor was nearly finished with the wall of scrambled egg.

'Ms Jocelyn,' Gabriel informed them, 'instructs me to tell you that Mr Dashiel is awake but continues to recuperate.'

'That's good,' said the Doctor, taking his tea from the tray Gabriel proffered. Martha sipped her tea, the hot, familiar flavour making her feel so much better. There was something brilliant about being so far in the future and still getting a dainty china cup of tea. However far into the past or future she went, she was constantly amazed how much people were just people, with the same worries and loves and things to eat. And that made it all the worse that Archibald had never had any of that. She looked over at him, where he was finding it difficult to get his cup of tea to fit round his long badger nose.

'Maybe you need a straw,' she said.

'Yeah,' said Archibald. He didn't seem to know what to make of the tea. Martha could see the wonder in his eyes at yet another, different flavour. She thought of all the things he would love to try for the first time: chips and chocolate and fruit and Sunday roasts. In a way she envied him.

'Right,' said the Doctor, prodding the soft scrambled egg with a finger. 'That's looking good.' He turned to Martha. 'Ladies first again?'

'No,' said Martha. 'We go through together this time.'

'OK,' said the Doctor. He turned to Archibald, Mrs Wingsworth and Gabriel. 'We'll just be a moment,' he told them. 'And then it should all be put right.'

'You mean, dear,' said Mrs Wingsworth appalled, 'you're leaving us behind?'

'Nah,' said the Doctor. 'This is going to be boring. But we need you here covering our backs.' Martha knew what he was really up to – keeping them safe from whatever dangers awaited. The crew, after all, were waiting to fight anyone coming through. 'Big responsibility that,' the Doctor went on. 'If you think you're up to it.'

'Of course we are!' said Mrs Wingsworth, so affronted she spilt some of her gin and tonic.

'Yeah,' agreed Archibald.'

'Mr Doctor,' said Gabriel. 'The crew may have instructions to shoot you if you enter the bridge without authority.'

'Yeah?' said the Doctor. 'Well I'm the only one of us who hasn't been killed yet. Probably my turn. See ya!'

And he grabbed Martha's hand and moved quickly forwards.

Again the scrambled egg pressed close against her, threatening to hold her fast. But Martha held the Doctor's hand tightly, and in a moment they were out the far side.

The bridge was a long, grey room with a horseshoe of computers at its centre, each computer at the command of a different tall, athletic human. Their tight grey uniforms showed off fine, sculpted muscles.

'Hello,' said the Doctor cheerily. 'I'm the Doctor…'

Still holding Martha's hand, he stepped forward into the room. And into an invisible wall of electricity. Martha didn't have time to scream as the energy tore through her. She just had time to feel the Doctor's hand burning up in hers, and then they were both gone.

NINE

'I've got my eyes shut,' she heard the Doctor say. 'Are you there yet?'

Martha opened her eyes. She was sat on the floor, her back against the cold and unyielding wall of scrambled egg, and facing the horseshoe of computers. The Doctor sat next to her, his eyes tightly closed. His suit was torn in places and blackened from where the invisible wall of electricity had cooked it. The skin around his nose and ears looked raw and pink and painful.

A thought struck Martha and she quickly lifted the hem of her vest top. The scar from the knife wound had gone.

'Yeah,' she said. 'I'm here.'

He opened his eyes and grinned at her. 'That was exciting,' he said, as if they'd just stepped off a rollercoaster.

'Yeah,' she said. 'But let's not make a habit of it.'

'Chicken,' he replied.

'Ahem,' said a new voice above them. Martha looked up to see a handsome bloke with a cool, handlebar moustache. He gazed sternly down at them from where he stood a couple of feet away, keeping the wall of killer electricity between them. His tight grey uniform only emphasised his impressive muscles.

'Um,' said Martha. 'Hi.'

'You survived,' he said, sounding disappointed. His voice was warm and rich, like in an advert for coffee.

'Sorry about that,' said the Doctor easily. 'Don't know what we were thinking.'

The handsome man turned back to his handsome colleagues. 'Captain,' he called. 'They survived.' Yeah, OK, thought Martha, people coming back from the dead was unusual. But for all he looked lovely, his voice was a bit whinging.

Martha turned to the Doctor, hoping he'd know what to do. They were trapped between the cold scrambled egg and the invisible wall of electricity. The Doctor pulled a face at her and shrugged. They would just have to see what happened next.

The tall, well-toned captain came over, one of those lucky women whose bone structure meant she could be anywhere between thirty-five and sixty. Her long, sleek hair was heavily layered and helped emphasise her cheekbones. It reminded Martha of the 'Rachel' look, fashionable when she'd been at university. It also reminded her of the kind of rich students who had so much time to spend on styling their hair.

'They're human,' said the captain, with surprise and another coffee-selling voice. Closer now, Martha could see the fine worry lines etched into the skin around her steely, determined eyes. She looked fierce and brave as well as beautiful.

'And so are you,' said the Doctor. He turned to Martha. 'I just knew there'd be some of your lot somewhere round the place. Doing your thing, all being in space. Just look at you! You're brilliant.'

'Doctor,' said Martha sternly. 'Don't do that, it's embarrassing.'

'Don't do what?' said the Doctor.

'That. Talking down to the Homo sapiens.'

'Sorry,' he said. And then he grinned. 'Though really, you're Homo sapiens *sapiens*. There's a whole sub-species thing. And you've got this—' He noticed the way she was looking at him, arms folded, one eyebrow raised. 'Sorry,' he said. He turned his attention to the starship's captain. 'I was just saying to your mate,' he said, 'how we didn't mean to live through your clever wossname. Can only apologise, really.'

The captain scrutinised the Doctor as if he wriggled in a test tube. 'He speaks standard,' she said. 'Of a sort.'

'What should I do with them?' said the handsome man beside her, stroking his handlebar moustache.

'Oh,' said the Doctor to Martha, making a great show of ignoring the two fearsome people standing right in front of them. 'I imagine they'll want to interrogate us. Find out what we know.'

'We do know a lot,' agreed Martha.

'We do,' said the Doctor. 'The war, the pirates, the experimental drive and what's gone wrong with it…' He looked up at the captain and grinned.

The captain bit her bottom lip as she considered. 'We could run the wall of electricity closer to the door,' she said simply. 'Fry them again.'

'It's really not going to make any difference,' said the Doctor. 'We're very hardy. Like dandelions.'

'We could shoot them, sir,' the handsome man suggested to the captain. In fact, he was so good-looking with his eyes and moustache and twinkling smile that Martha didn't really mind too much about what he was suggesting. She supposed people were always going to be better looking in the future, just as she'd found Shakespeare a bit unwashed and smelly. Oh, she thought; perhaps this handsome bloke looked at her, a girl from the distant past, with the same kind of horror.

'Or you could say how helpful it is to have someone turn up who knows what's going on,' said the Doctor.

'What *is* going on?' the captain asked him. She didn't, Martha noted, try to use her beauty on him. Her good looks were a side issue to the job in hand. The captain expected to be taken seriously.

'Well,' said the Doctor. 'Why don't you let us out of this thing and then we can chat about it?'

The captain considered. 'I suppose they are human,' she said, as if humans had never done anything bad, ever.

'Captain?' asked the handsome man.

'Let them out,' the captain told the handsome man. 'But keep them covered.'

Two other handsome men in uniform hurried over with elegant, little guns, which they trained on the Doctor and Martha. The handsome man nodded to one of his well-toned colleagues working at the horseshoe of computers. The colleague, a beautiful brunette, operated some of the controls in front of her, but nothing much seemed to happen as far as Martha could tell. Still, the handsome man beckoned her forward.

'Come on,' he said. 'Move.'

With the guns pointing at her, Martha made to move forward but the Doctor grabbed her hand.

'I'll go first,' he said, and took a step through the space where the wall of electricity had been. Nothing happened to him. He looked himself up and down, just to be on the safe side, then looked back at Martha, smiling. 'Easy,' he said.

The bridge was more like an office than the control deck of a spaceship, thought Martha as she stepped forward. There was no big view screen or anything like that. Instead the handsome, uniformed people each had a place at the horseshoe of computers. Each individual computer screen was also projected onto the wall behind the person manning it, so everyone could see what everyone else was up to. For a moment Martha thought this meant they couldn't get away with skiving – there'd be no online shopping or Facebook when everyone else could look round at your screen. But then she realised that the captain need only stand in the gap of the horseshoe to see all the wall screens at once.

The Doctor was gazing at the wall screens, too, lapping up all the information. His eyes flicked from screen to screen, comparing the different sets of data. One screen showed a complex bar graph all in different colours, another, which held the Doctor's attention, showed some kind of blobby spaceship out in space. It looked, thought Martha, like a giant, spiky peach, the spikes all kinds of guns and space weaponry.

'That's beautiful!' enthused the Doctor.

'The pirate vessel?' asked the captain – like Martha, she thought it really ugly. A spherical pod jutting from the front of the peach seemed to be the badger pirates' bridge and living quarters, and two small bumps on either side of the peach looked like nippy little engines. From the back, there was what looked like a frozen plume of spray, hundreds of tiny droplets frozen in an instant. Martha realised with a start that each droplet was a boarding capsule, like the one that had brought Archibald, Dashiel and Jocelyn aboard.

'No,' laughed the Doctor. 'The stasis wave in between us and the ship. Seen a few of 'em in my time, of course. But that one's just a corker.'

The captain, the handsome man beside her and Martha all scrutinised the wall screen that showed the pirate ship.

'I can't see anything,' said Martha.

'No?' said the Doctor. 'Try these?' He handed her his glasses. She put them on, but everything was a blur.

'I think,' said Martha, handing him back the glasses, 'this is going to be one of those last-of-the-you-know-what things.'

'Nah,' said the Doctor. 'You just need to widen your perspective. Captain, you wanna set your screens to show Kodicek fluctuations of zero point one and bigger.'

The captain nodded to the slender brunette working at the horseshoe of computers, who worked one of the controls. There was a gasp from those watching the screens. Where the pirate ship and its plume of boarding vessels had looked frozen in time, now they could see it caught in the tendrils of a twinkling, pink-blue haze. The computers added lines through the haze, like the pattern iron filings made around a magnet.

'We're at the heart of it,' explained the Doctor, pointing out how the contours were packed more closely together nearer their own position. 'They're just on the periphery.' When no one responded he added, 'That just means the edge.'

'And it's atemporal mismatch?' asked the captain. It was funny, thought Martha, but there was something about the Doctor that people always trusted, especially those in authority. He had a way of talking to them at their level. No, it wasn't trust, she realised. They saw he could be useful, like he could do their homework for them.

'Yeah,' said the Doctor. 'At least, it's your computers'

representation of it. You find yourself facing the stuff close up, it looks like cold scrambled egg. And feels a lot like it, too.'

'Suggestions?' the captain asked her crew, as if retaking charge. Martha could see the Doctor torn between butting in with the right answer and hearing what the humans had to say.

'Some kind of temporal leak,' suggested the brunette. 'A side effect of the drive.'

'Perhaps the pirate ship is just occupying the point of space-time we wanted to pass through,' said another.

'Or they've got some kind of repulsion device that negates the effects of the drive,' said someone else.

The captain considered these suggestions, then turned to the Doctor. 'I suppose you have your own ideas?' she asked.

'Oh yeah,' said the Doctor. 'But you were all doing so well!' And then he knotted his eyebrows together. 'I'm sorry, I don't know your name.'

'I'm Captain Georgina Wet-Eleven, Second Mid Dynasty.'

'Hello Captain Georgina,' said the Doctor, shaking her warmly by the hand. 'I'm the Doctor and this is my friend—'

'Thank you,' said Captain Georgina sourly. 'I got your names before.' She glanced quickly at Martha. Martha, not really sure what else to do, rolled her eyes, as if the Doctor was always like this. Which he was. But the gesture didn't seem to go down too well with the captain, who remained entirely stony faced. Martha felt a bit silly.

'I'm waiting, Doctor,' Captain Georgina said. 'You were going to explain what happened.'

'Oh yeah, that,' said the Doctor airily. 'Well let's start from first principles. You were flying along, minding your own business, and then these pirates attacked you.'

'Correct,' said Captain Georgina.

'Only,' said the Doctor, 'you've got this clever new drive you can use, so you give the order.'

'It hadn't been tested before,' said the captain. 'But in the circumstances it seemed the best thing to do.'

'Well, yeah,' said the Doctor. He leaned forward, speaking softly. 'You've got the safety of the passengers to think about, haven't you, captain?'

The captain snorted, wrinkling her nose at him prettily. 'What are you insinuating?' she said.

'Me?' said the Doctor. 'Nothing. I wouldn't know how. Anyway, you stick the drive on as quick as you can – but not before one pirate capsule has already got here. And there's a whopping great bang and you're all stuck in this room. Yeah?'

'What makes you think that we're stuck in the room?' said Captain Georgina.

'Oh,' said the Doctor, glancing back at the wall of cold scrambled egg that blocked the door back out to the sleeping quarters. 'Er, have you tried the doors?'

The man with the moustache who had first accosted

them went over to the doors. He prodded then punched then shot at the wall of cold scrambled egg. It did not yield to him.

'We're trapped!' he said, with that same note of whinging that Martha had noticed before. He might look all handsome, she thought, but he'd drive you mad as a boyfriend.

'Phew,' said the Doctor. 'That could have been embarrassing.'

'What is this material?' asked Captain Georgina, her eyes narrowed with concern.

'Well,' said the Doctor.

'It stops you getting out the door,' said Martha.

The Doctor laughed. 'You and your technical explanations!' he said.

'I see,' said Captain Georgina. 'But that is hardly a problem. The transmat remains operational.' She indicated the booth in one corner of the room, the twin of the one Martha had seen all that time ago in the starship's engine rooms.

'Doctor!' she said, stopping herself from saying more, that now they could get back to the TARDIS. Captain Georgina didn't need to know such detail.

'Yes,' said the Doctor. 'Have you tried the transmat in the last day or so?' he asked the captain.

'I used it this morning,' said the handsome man with the moustache. 'I noted no discrepancies or errors.' He couldn't help, though, glancing down at himself just to check that he was all there. Martha shuddered at the thought of what would happen if there was a problem when you were in the middle of transmatting yourself somewhere.

'Oh,' said the Doctor, looking confused. 'That's a bit of a surprise. I thought it wouldn't be working.'

But a thought had struck Martha. 'How long's it been since the pirates attacked?'

The pretty brunette checked the read-out on the screen in front of her. 'Four minutes and fourteen seconds,' she said.

The Doctor was grinning at Martha. 'Oh, that's brilliant,' he said to her. 'We're in a different pocket of time because of the wall of scrambled egg. So it's been hours and hours for the rest of the ship, and just four minutes... twenty-two seconds up here!'

'Which is why they haven't checked the doors or whether the transmat works,' said Martha.

'You're saying,' said Captain Georgina gravely, 'that we're sand-banked in time?'

'Oh, good analogy!' cooed the Doctor. 'I'm adding that one to the list. Yes, the *Brilliant* is sand-banked in time, and so it's like the rest of the universe is frozen. Which is what you see on your screens. In fact, they're just carrying on as usual and you're the ones who look like you disappeared.'

The crew considered this. 'It could offer a major tactical advantage,' suggested the handsome man.

'Possibly,' said the captain.

'Well not really,' said the Doctor. 'You can't move like

this, can you? Can't do anything, really. Except make conversation and eat canapés.'

'Have you got any canapés?' Martha asked the handsome man with the handlebar moustache.

'Not here,' he told her. 'But they have them in the cocktail lounge. Which apparently we can't get to.'

'No,' said Martha. 'Sorry about that. I'm Martha by the way.'

'Thomas,' said the handsome man. 'Er. Aide-to-Captain Thomas Five-Shoelace, Slow Station Settlement.'

'Aw,' said the Doctor. 'I've been to Slow Station. Did the thing of jumping off the orbital tower and free-falling to the surface!'

'I think everyone does that,' said Thomas.

'All right,' said Captain Georgina, impatiently. 'I think your explanation matches the available evidence and what we know about the experimental drive. Even if it is unusual.'

'Yeah well,' said the Doctor. 'Experimental drives don't act like you expect them to. That's why they're experimental.'

'Thank you, Doctor,' said the captain. 'My main concern is what we do to free ourselves from the sand-bank.'

'Ah well,' said the Doctor. 'Strictly speaking, you don't.'

Captain Georgina was about to ask him why not when there was a crash from the wall of cold scrambled egg.

Three rough-looking, space-suited, helmeted figures charged through the eggy material and came clattering onto the bridge. Their spacesuits were battered and battle-worn, with a skull and crossbones daubed on each of their chests. It took a moment for Martha to recognise the three badger pirates, because they'd put on their helmets.

'Doctor!' said Dashiel, his voice echoing because of the helmet. 'Fort you must 'ave died!'

'Sorry to disappoint you,' said the Doctor. 'How long have you been waiting for us?'

'Er,' said Dashiel. 'Dunno. Coupla days.'

'Sorry,' said the Doctor. 'Got chatting.'

'Who are these people?' asked Captain Georgina, maintaining an impressive air of calm. No, thought Martha, the captain was sneering at the intruders, like they weren't good enough to be in the same room. Around her, Martha saw, the other humans had raised their own elegant, little guns.

'Well,' said the Doctor. 'They used to be pirates, but we've been having words. That's Dashiel, Jocelyn and Archibald.'

'Allo,' said Archibald, waving a hairy paw.

'I see,' said Captain Georgina. 'They do seem to be carrying guns.'

'Oh yeah,' said the Doctor. 'But don't worry about that. I disarmed them hours ago—'

As he spoke, Thomas erupted in a plume of brilliant pink light. He had barely enough time to scream before he had been entirely consumed.

'Ah,' said the Doctor, scratching at his jaw. 'That really shouldn't have happened.'

'They started workin' again,' Dashiel explained, as he shot the brunette who still worked at the horseshoe of computers.

'Oh yeah,' said the Doctor. 'I should have thought of that. The loop affects the guns as well.'

'Fire at will!' cried Captain Georgina. 'Repel the invaders!'

'Wait!' cried the Doctor. 'Wait!'

One of the uniformed men dived forward, firing his elegant little gun into the attacking badgers. A blast of bright white energy smashed into Dashiel, hurling him back into the wall of scrambled egg. His broken body lay steaming on the ground.

'Huh,' said Archibald as he fired back at the uniformed man. The man was consumed in pink light. Archibald and Jocelyn ran forward, using the horseshoe of computers as cover while they fought the rallying humans.

'Oh, this is just silly!' said the Doctor. He grabbed Martha's hand and they rushed to the only other shelter – the transmat booth set into the wall. The door opened easily, and the Doctor locked it after them with his sonic screwdriver.

'You've got to stop them!' said Martha.

The Doctor was watching the fire fight closely. Captain Georgina and her men were caught with nowhere to hide. They fought back valiantly, but it was easy for

Archibald and Jocelyn to pick them off one by one. Martha felt a little dizzy, her eyes blinded by so much brilliant pink and white light.

Yet the Doctor seemed to find it all fascinating. 'How did they get through the wall?' he asked, as if watching some scientific experiment and not a room of people being killed.

'Doctor, they're wiping each other out!' said Martha.

'Oh yeah,' said the Doctor easily. 'They're bound to. But then they'll just wake up again.' He turned to look at her, then seemed more taken by the controls of the transmat. 'That's funny,' he said.

'Oh, it's hilarious,' muttered Martha as she watched another couple of uniformed men eaten up by pink light. There was just Captain Georgina and one of her men left, curled up close to the far side of the horseshoe of computers, just out of sight of the badgers.

'Thomas was right,' said the Doctor, still scrutinising the transmat controls. 'This hasn't been used in hours. You couldn't use it anyway. The delay between the two booths would just tear you apart. No way out, I'm afraid.'

'Doctor!' said Martha through gritted teeth, as Archibald reached round the horseshoe to shoot the man beside Captain Georgina.

'Well, that *is* funny,' said the Doctor. 'Because when we were down in the engine rooms, something was trying to get through. Which means, since Thomas went and came back again already, that whoever we saw arriving hasn't set off from here yet.' He seemed to notice Martha wasn't paying him any attention, and looked back at the fighting.

Jocelyn and Archibald were creeping round the sides of the horseshoe of computers, while Captain Georgina, alone now, waited for them to reach her. She cradled the elegant little gun in her hands. After a moment Martha realised she wasn't just cradling it, she was working controls in the handle.

'Gotcha!' said Archibald, leaping out at her and firing. From the far side of the computers, Jocelyn was leaping too, keen not to miss out on the kill.

But before the pink energy hit Captain Georgina she exploded in white light. The blast tore through the horseshoe of computers, screens and keyboards shattering all around. Jocelyn disappeared behind the explosions. Archibald's body was sent tumbling across the room, so that he smashed into the door of the transmat booth and lay still. Martha reached for the handle of the door, but it wouldn't open.

'I have to help him,' she said quietly.

'You can in a minute,' said the Doctor, busy again with the controls of the transmat.

'They've killed each other,' said Martha so quietly she barely heard herself.

The Doctor turned to her, put a hand on her shoulder. 'Yes,' he said. 'But they'll be fine again in a minute.'

'But they'll just get up and start fighting again,' she said. 'It's so stupid!'

'I know,' said the Doctor gently, his eyes looking deeply into hers. And then he grinned. 'Which is why we'll have to be really clever if we're going stop them.'

'Oh,' she said. 'You've got a plan.'

'Yes,' he said. 'And, even if I say so myself, it's really quite a good one.'

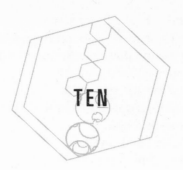

TEN

The Doctor pointed the sonic screwdriver at the door of the transmat booth, and with a click the door unlocked. The moment it opened, Martha was assaulted by an appalling stink of death and burnt fabric. She stepped carefully over Archibald's smoking body, following the Doctor over to the smashed and still burning horseshoe of computers.

She glanced back and Archibald's body had vanished. Martha knew he'd be coming back, that all the humans and badgers would be resurrected. And yet it didn't make her feel any less sick at having watched them slaughter one other. She felt again the cold steel blade that had killed her earlier that day. The time loop on the *Brilliant* brought them back from the dead, but it didn't stop violence and pain.

The Doctor fussed with the horseshoe of computers, the keyboards and screens all suddenly just as they had been before the badgers attacked. Then, happy with whatever he'd done, he collected up the scattered guns and weapons and set to work on them with the sonic screwdriver. He had that serious, single-minded look in his eyes he often got when tinkering.

'Anything I can do?' she asked.

'Um,' he said, glancing quickly round. 'Don't think so. But it's nice of you to ask.'

She stuck her hands in the pockets of her jeans and walked slowly round the horseshoe of computers. For all she was bored, she had the eerie feeling of all sorts of activity going on wherever she wasn't quite looking. There were bodies and wreckage strewn across the floor, but she'd glance away and then it would be tidy. It was just easier to close her eyes and count slowly up to ten.

When she opened them, everything was better. The bridge was clean and gleaming, the mess all taken care of. In front of the door blocked by the wall of scrambled egg sat the human crew and the three badger pirates. The badgers took off their helmets. Archibald waved at her with a hairy paw.

Beside him sat Thomas, the handsome man with the handlebar moustache. His uniform had charred and torn in a way which made him even more good-looking. Thomas tried to punch Archibald on the end of his wet black nose, but his fist struck what seemed to be an invisible wall of rubber, and bounced back to smack himself hard in the face.

'Oh yeah,' said the Doctor, still busy with what had once been a heap of guns. 'You want to look out for that.

I've messed with your wall of electricity and now it's not going to kill you. But you'll stay in your individual little pockets of it until you promise to behave.'

'Promise!' said Archibald immediately.

The Doctor adjusted a control and Archibald scampered free, joining Martha and the Doctor at the computers.

'But that's not fair!' protested Captain Georgina, as if he'd confiscated her sweets.

'Life's not fair,' Martha told her. 'Didn't your mother tell you?'

'Doctor,' said Captain Georgina gravely, completely ignoring Martha. 'You must be aware that the penalty for hijacking a starship is summary execution.'

The Doctor didn't even look up from his work on the former guns. So Martha took it on herself to answer for them both. 'You already killed us,' she said. 'So I think we're even, yeah?'

The captain held Martha's gaze, her eyes blazing with purest fury. 'You,' said Captain Georgina. 'Will. Release. Me. Now.' She spoke so carefully, so calmly, with such menace that it gave Martha goose bumps.

'Sorry,' said the Doctor airily. He finished whatever he'd made from the guns and came round the side of the horseshoe of computers to address his prisoners. 'Look, we got off to a bad start before. You seemed to be under the impression that you lot were in charge.' He grinned. 'Now are you going to play nicely?'

Dashiel and Jocelyn both promised to behave and

were duly released. The humans, taking their lead from Captain Georgina, sat where they were saying nothing. They looked, thought Martha, like a row of big sulky children.

'You're just going to leave them on the naughty step?' asked Martha.

'Have you got a better idea?' asked the Doctor, busy with his work.

'We could kill 'em,' suggested Dashiel.

'That is a possibility,' said the Doctor. 'But let's not, eh? Why don't you tell me how you three got in here? You've not got sonic screwdrivers, have you?'

'Nah,' said Dashiel. 'Archie told us what we 'ad to do.'

'Yeah,' said Archie proudly. 'You said. Vibrations.' He pronounced the last word carefully, like he was worried he might break it.

'Well, technically,' said the Doctor, 'it's resonance, but we'll let that pass. So what did you do?'

'Told Gabriel to make it vibrate,' said Jocelyn.

'And he just did as he was told?' asked Martha. She had learnt Gabriel had a very literal mind, and you needed to ask him things precisely.

'Nah,' said Archibald. 'He din't. So we asked Mrs Wingsworth.'

'I see,' said the Doctor. 'Clever.'

'We 'ad to say "please" and "thank you",' explained Dashiel. 'But then she told the robot.'

'You see?' said the Doctor. 'You just have to ask nicely.'

'Yeah,' said Dashiel, his eyes full of wonder at this amazing strategy.

'So Gabriel, what, vibrated,' said Martha, 'and then you could all get through?'

'He made a thing like yours,' explained Dashiel, pointing to the Doctor's top pocket, where he kept the sonic screwdriver. 'Made from broken guns.'

'He's a smart cookie, that Gabriel,' said the Doctor. 'Your guns are full of all sorts of aiming and power accessories. You know what I've just made out of them?'

'No,' said Dashiel.

The Doctor showed them the peculiar hotchpotch of wires and circuits he'd been working on when they awoke. 'It'll be a Teasmade when it's finished.'

Martha wanted to laugh at the looks on the badgers' faces – they were so impressed with everything. And the Doctor just lived to show off the whole time, so they made the perfect audience.

'Do you even know what a Teasmade is?' she asked them.

'Er,' said Dashiel, 'no.'

'Makes tea?' asked Archibald.

'That's right,' said the Doctor.

'Tea is good,' Archibald explained to his comrades.

'And if I can get the timer to work,' explained the Doctor, 'you can set it in advance. So you put it on before you go to bed and it wakes you in the morning with a fresh cup of tea.'

'But won't the guns just repair themselves when the loop works?' asked Martha.

'Maybe,' said the Doctor. 'But I'm hoping the ship will recognise that I've made them into something more useful.'

The badgers nodded, wide-eyed at this genius. Then Dashiel put out a hairy paw and touched the back of the Doctor's hand. 'We fort you'd been killed,' he said. He spoke gruffly, trying to cover up the real feeling in his voice. Despite everything they'd been through, despite all the pirates had done, Martha felt her heart go out to them.

'You came to rescue us,' she said.

'Yeah,' said Archibald. 'Kind of.'

'You came to avenge our deaths,' said the Doctor more sternly.

'Yeah,' said Dashiel.

'But you know better than that, don't you,' said the Doctor. 'Is revenge a good thing or a bad thing?'

'Good!' said Archibald with enthusiasm. Dashiel nudged him in the ribs. 'Er, bad,' said Archibald.

'But why?' said Martha to Dashiel and Jocelyn. 'Last time I saw you, you wanted me dead.'

'Yeah,' said Jocelyn. 'Sorry 'bout that.'

'But Archie said,' explained Dashiel. 'How you're good. How you let us eat the food.'

'An' we were bored,' added Archie. 'What?' he said, when Dashiel nudged him again.

'You're not really taking their side over ours, are

you?' said Captain Georgina from over by the wall of scrambled egg. She had got to her feet and stood with her hands pressed against the invisible rubber wall, so that she looked like she was performing some not very ambitious mime. The humans were all beautiful, well-toned and glamorous, but imprisoned they all looked awkward and unsure, and a bit silly. 'They're stupid, clumsy animals,' Captain Georgina continued. 'And they smell disgusting.'

The badgers bristled. 'We're not stupid,' said Dashiel.

'Now, now,' said the Doctor to the captain, wagging his index finger at her. 'That's not very nice is it? Look where your airs and graces have got you so far.'

'What do you mean?' asked Captain Georgina. 'These things are *made* to be inferior.'

'Yeah,' admitted Dashiel, shrugging.

'I don't understand,' said Martha. 'You mean this lot made the badgers?'

'Well, not this lot specifically,' the Doctor told her. 'Your lot generally. Humans. You didn't think it odd what the badgers are wearing? Uniforms with a skull and crossbones. *Human* skulls. Shows who's really in charge.'

Martha couldn't believe her ears. 'You mean they're slaves,' she said. 'Like the mouthless men down in the engine rooms?'

'Oh, they don't call them slaves,' said the Doctor. 'But you need someone to do the dirty work for you. You get into space and it's no longer immigrants but Ood and Monoids and Vocs.' He gestured towards Captain

Georgina and her staff. 'And then this lot are growing their own. Hands in the engine rooms who won't answer back and badgers to do all their thieving.'

'It's disgusting,' said Martha.

'We did not make the badgers!' Captain Georgina protested.

'No,' said the Doctor, darkly. 'But your species did. Some rival gang or faction from just down the street. Someone who's seen the war coming.'

'Yeah,' said Jocelyn. Dashiel glared at her.

'We dun't talk 'bout the client,' said Archibald. 'It's con-fiden'-shawl.' Again he spoke the last word with great care.

'Oh that's right,' said the Doctor. 'You've gotta protect your clients. Imagine how embarrassed they'd be if anyone found out what they were up to!'

'Yeah,' said Dashiel, though he didn't seem quite sure what he had just agreed with. Martha could see his brain struggling to understand.

'They don't own you,' she told him. 'No one owns anyone.'

'Hah!' laughed Dashiel, and then his eyes narrowed as he realised it wasn't a joke.

'How can something like this happen?' she asked the Doctor. 'How can it be allowed to happen?'

'You really want to know?' asked the Doctor.

'No,' said Dashiel earnestly.

'Yes,' said Martha. 'We have to face this stuff.'

'People like this lot,' said the Doctor, waving a hand

at the imprisoned human crew and not quite including Martha with them, 'live like the whole universe is there solely for their entertainment. They trash their own planet and, despite years of evidence and warnings, all kinds of species die out.'

'Badgers,' said Jocelyn quietly.

'Yeah,' the Doctor admitted. 'I'm sorry.'

'S'OK,' said Jocelyn.

'But not all the humans were the same,' said the Doctor. 'There are ones who were different and cared. And they did their best to gather loads of DNA records and set up a library of all the extinct species they could. One day, they said, humanity would know better and then they could recreate all the wildlife.'

'So why didn't they?' asked Martha. 'Why not make the badgers like badgers used to be?'

'Ah,' said the Doctor. 'On some worlds they did. But not on very many.'

'Ain't no profit, is there?' said Dashiel, shrugging.

'They were much more useful as badger-human mixes,' said the Doctor. 'Then they could be sent out to work.'

'That's…' said Martha. 'It's so bad I don't know what it is.'

'It's market forces,' stated Captain Georgina, from over by the door.

'These three,' said the Doctor, indicating the badgers, 'get their genes from the Western European badger, like the ones you'd get in England. Dies out in your lifetime.'

He grinned. 'The Latin name for the Western European badger is *Meles meles meles*. I always liked that one! So I guess the human/badger mash-up would be *Homo sapiens sapiens meles meles meles*!' Martha just eyed him wearily. 'Oh,' said the Doctor. 'Well, I think that's funny, even if no one else does.'

'I'm sorry,' Martha told the badgers. She thought of the miserable lives that these badger pirates had had, where simple things like cheese and tea seemed like amazing wonders.

'She's right though,' said Dashiel, gesturing towards Captain Georgina. 'We ain't as good as them.'

'See?' said Captain Georgina. 'They know that we're better. So it's not right to keep us locked up.'

'Better?' laughed the Doctor. 'They caught you in their spaceship, despite your clever disguise. They stopped you before you could use the experimental drive. And now they're free and you're not. So who's got most points?'

Captain Georgina glowered at him, but she said nothing further.

'What disguise?' asked Martha. 'You said they had a disguise.'

'Oh,' said the Doctor. 'The *Brilliant* isn't a luxury cruiser. The crew here clearly don't give a stuff about the passengers. It's the robots that are programmed to look after them.'

'It's a cover,' said Martha, horrified. 'You were using them as a shield. It's just about the experimental drive!'

'That is a security issue,' said Captain Georgina testily. She seemed small and impotent where she stood, the cage that held her not even visible. 'I can neither confirm nor deny the allegation.'

'Bet you wouldn't have tested the experimental drive if the passengers had been humans,' said the Doctor.

Captain Georgina bridled at this. 'There's a war coming,' she said. 'Billions of people's lives are at stake. There have to be priorities.'

'As long as they're not your sort,' Martha said to her, utterly disgusted.

'*Our* sort,' corrected Captain Georgina. 'You're humans, too.'

'Lucky us,' said Martha. The Doctor ignored the captain, busy again with the controls. Martha, though, couldn't turn her back on the captain. She felt she had to stare her down, making her look away first. As if that would somehow win the moral point.

'I don't like it either, but it had to be done,' said Captain Georgina eventually. And she looked away.

Martha joined the Doctor and Dashiel at the horseshoe of computers. Dashiel seemed transfixed by the screen that showed the spiky, peach-shaped pirate spaceship. 'Can we call the *Mandelbrot* from 'ere?' he asked the Doctor.

The Doctor laughed. 'Is that what your ship is called?' he asked.

'The *Mandelbrot Sett*,' said Dashiel. 'Yeah.'

'It's a pun!' laughed the Doctor.

'No,' said Dashiel. 'It's a spaceship.'

'Well anyway,' said the Doctor. 'You can't call them. We're still subject to the stasis field. They're in another time zone entirely.'

Dashiel considered this. 'Good,' he said.

'Captain Florence is scary,' explained Archibald. 'An' she won't like any of this stuff.'

'We can stay 'ere,' said Jocelyn.

'What, for ever?' asked Martha.

'Yeah,' said Archie. 'We brung food.' He rummaged in the front of his spacesuit and withdrew a silver tray. Dashiel and Jocelyn also had silver trays tucked into their spacesuits, and they placed the three trays down on the horseshoe of computers.

'Count to somethin',' said Dashiel, closing his eyes tightly. 'One… um, *another* one…'

Martha looked to the Doctor, who had also closed his eyes. When she looked back at the trays they were filled with canapés. Archibald had brought the tray that held infinite cheese and pineapple sticks. He offered them to Martha.

'Thank you,' she said.

When Archibald had offered the tray to the Doctor and his two comrades, he headed over to the human crew, still imprisoned by the door. He prodded the invisible wall of rubber with his hairy paw, then looked back at the Doctor.

'Are you sure about this?' asked the Doctor, surprised.

'Yeah,' said Archibald.

'And what about you, captain?' the Doctor asked Captain Georgina.

The captain was staring at Archibald, just a foot in front of her. Her expression was impossible to read. And then, to Martha's amazement, the captain simply sighed.

'We can agree to a truce,' she said. 'There's not much else we can do.'

'Brilliant!' said the Doctor and worked the controls. Captain Georgina reached out a hand tentatively, expecting to still meet the invisible wall of rubber. She lifted one cheese and pineapple stick from Archibald's tray, then nodded to him curtly.

'Thank you,' she said.

'You take 'em,' said Archibald, pressing the whole tray into her hands. 'I'll get the blini pizzas.'

He hurried back to the horseshoe of computer desks, and so missed seeing what he'd just achieved. Captain Georgina held the tray of cheese and pineapple sticks and, without thinking about it, offered them to Thomas, stood beside her. Martha could see the look in his eyes – it wouldn't do to refuse the captain. So he took a cheese and pineapple stick, and soon the captain was serving all the crew. Archibald hurried back with the tray of blinis, and Jocelyn joined him with the tray of sausage rolls. Soon a pleasant little party atmosphere was going. And since the badgers and the captain were serving the food, it seemed nobody quite dared question why they weren't fighting any more.

'They're all friends,' said Martha, amazed. She turned to the Doctor, who was busy with the computers.

'Yeah,' he said, not looking up. 'If they can't kill each other they might as well just get along. At least until something happens to change the status quo.' His long skinny fingers danced across the controls, the information on the screens changing too rapidly for Martha to keep up.

'What is it?' she said.

'Go and have some canapés,' he told her.

'Oh,' she said. 'That bad?'

'It is quite bad,' he said.

'What is it?' asked Captain Georgina, coming over with an empty tray in her hands. Archibald also had an empty tray, and it seemed he was going to show her the method for making it full again.

'Oh, nothing,' said the Doctor easily.

Captain Georgina glanced at the screens. 'We're eating up energy,' she said.

'Eating is good,' said Archibald.

'Yes,' said the Doctor. 'But the time loop isn't perfect. It's got a gap in it.'

'So it's more like a horseshoe than a loop,' said Martha, seeing the horseshoe of computers right in front of her.

'Yeah, OK,' said the Doctor. 'Enough with the analogies. So we come speeding round the loop and hit the gap. But the *Brilliant* has stuff that knows how to bend reality, so it guides us back to the other side and round we go again.'

'And when it's doing that, it restocks the nibbles and brings us back to life,' said Martha.

'All part of the first-class service,' said the Doctor. 'But each time it does that, it needs a bit of power to push it round again. Only it's not a bit of power. It's quite a lot.'

'But we don't have power reserves like this,' said Captain Georgina, her eyes never leaving the screens. 'That's more than a ship this size could ever hope to contain.'

'Ah well,' said the Doctor. 'Depends how you look at it. You know how much energy is freed up just by being stood still in time? You're stuck in the space between moments, so it's like you're idling. Plenty of reserves just because none of you are really moving.'

'So we're OK?' said Martha, relieved. For a moment, she'd thought they were in danger.

'Oh yeah,' said the Doctor breezily. 'Well, kind of.'

'Good,' said Archibald.

'When you say kind of,' said Martha. 'You mean we *are* in danger.'

'Yeah,' he admitted.

'The energy needed keeps increasing,' said Captain Georgina, studying the screens.

'Does it?' asked Archibald.

'It does,' said the Doctor. 'You see, you're all using up energy while you're stuck here. Breathing, eating, talking, shooting. And coming back from the dead. It all has to come from somewhere.'

'What will happen?' asked Martha. She didn't like how calmly he was taking it. Usually, just a sniff of trouble was enough to get him all fidgety and excited. It also didn't help that behind them the other badgers and humans were enjoying nibbles and polite conversation. She struggled to take it seriously.

'Well,' said the Doctor, sticking his hands in his trouser pockets. 'There'll come a point where the energy isn't there. It'll hit the gap and there won't be enough momentum to get back round again.'

'So we'll be free?' said Martha.

The Doctor jutted out his jaw. 'In a manner of speaking.'

'We *won't* be free of the time loop?' she asked him.

'We'll be dead,' said Captain Georgina. 'The whole starship will implode.'

'Yeah,' said the Doctor. 'Something of that sort.'

'But there must be something we can do!' said Martha.

'Well yeah,' said the Doctor. 'There's always something. I think I could correct the problem, get us off the sand-bank.'

'So do it!' said Martha.

'Ah,' said the Doctor. 'Still a problem after that.'

'Captain Florence dun't take pris'ners,' said Archibald.

'I'd sort of suspected that,' said the Doctor. 'So that's why it's tricky. If I don't get us out of this, we're all going to die. But if I do, the pirate ship is waiting.'

ELEVEN

The human crew continued to eat canapés, chat and ignore their inevitable doom. Martha couldn't bear even to watch them. She could feel her own heart beating, a sudden sense of herself being alive, of wanting to *be* alive.

She looked round at the Doctor, busy at the controls of the transmat booth, trying to make it do anything that might help them. He'd used the sonic screwdriver, he'd also used his fists. Nothing seemed to be working. But he kept at it, and she started to think he was just trying to keep himself busy. So he wouldn't have time to think about being trapped. So he wouldn't have to meet her eye.

Martha couldn't help but think back to what the Doctor had said in the TARDIS, when she'd been begging him to bring them here. He'd said there were rules, that they couldn't get involved and they couldn't change anything. And now the two of them were caught up in the same fate as everyone else.

It could be brilliant, flitting through all time and space meeting all kinds of people. But Martha had seen enough people killed, enough terrible, awful things, to know their travels came with a price. And she'd known there was going to be trouble on the *Brilliant* – that it was going to disappear. The humans and badgers and Mrs Wingsworth had been doomed even before the Doctor set the controls of the TARDIS... And now she and the Doctor were doomed with them.

She made her way over to him. 'You can't get us out of this,' she said. 'Even if you get that thing working.'

He looked up at her. 'Can't I?'

'It would change history,' said Martha. 'And you can't do that. You said there were rules.'

'Rules?' asked Captain Georgina, coming to join them. She seemed to be taking everyone's certain deaths quite easily. Perhaps, thought Martha, it would make her look less effortlessly beautiful if she allowed herself to panic. Or perhaps she just knew there was nothing she could do. Martha's dad always said you should only worry about stuff you actually had any control over. The other stuff would just happen anyway. It was what he usually said when he was arguing with Martha's mum.

'Well, not rules as such,' said the Doctor. 'We have responsibilities. You see, we're sort of from the future and the *Brilliant* disappeared.'

'I see,' said Captain Georgina.

'You do?' said the Doctor. Martha knew he enjoyed it

when people freaked out about time travel.

'I'm fully briefed on the implications of the experimental drive,' said the captain. 'It stands to reason where this technology was leading. I assume you've come back to fix the problem for us.'

'Um,' said the Doctor. 'Yeah, well I was gonna see what we could do.'

Captain Georgina nodded. 'Then we sit and wait it out,' she said.

'Well, yes,' said the Doctor. 'But that's not what Martha was asking. Not *can* we get out of this, but if we could, then *should* we?'

'You're telling us it's wrong?' asked Captain Georgina.

'Wrong is bad,' said Archibald, coming over with a tray of blinis.

'So is it wrong to tamper with reality like that?' said the Doctor. 'To come back from the dead?'

'The experimental drive causes problems with causality anyway,' said Captain Georgina. 'Even just starting it up affects what we think of as reality.'

'That's right,' said the Doctor. 'But that's not just true of your clever engine. Look, you change history just by doing anything. Or *not* doing anything. What you do, what you strive for, every choice you ever make. That's what builds the future.'

'But you only get one go at it,' said Martha. 'Normally, I mean. If you get it wrong, that's tough.'

'You have to deal with the consequences of what you

do,' said the Doctor.

'Aw,' said Archibald. 'Do we 'ave to?'

'Yes,' said the Doctor. 'It's called being a grown-up.'

'Sounds really boring,' said Archibald.

'Sometimes it would be good to be able go back and do things again,' admitted Martha.

'You'd think so, wouldn't you?' said the Doctor gravely. 'But it doesn't work like that. It's like telling lies. You can never just tell the one fib, can you? Sooner or later you've got to tell another, just to back up the first one. A week later, you're juggling a whole intricate patchwork of lies on lies on lies. You can't remember what you've told different people, and you're probably not entirely sure what the real version is any more. So it's only a matter of time before someone catches you out or you just plain forget something and it all collapses, boom!'

'I've an ex-boyfriend you should explain that to,' said Martha.

'Before or after he's an ex?' he said.

For a moment Martha could see the Doctor turning up on a rainy night in 2005 and sorting out one particular row. 'OK,' she said, unsettled by what she'd just been offered. 'It's just a world of messy and complicated, yeah?'

'That's it,' said the Doctor. 'I hate all that tricky continuity stuff.'

'We just have to accept the hand we're dealt,' said Captain Georgina.

'No cheating,' said Archibald.

'Well…' said the Doctor, and his eyes glittered. 'Our real problem is how we get out of this mess *without* changing history. Which needs us to be very clever indeed. If only we had someone with an innate understanding of the space-time continuum. Someone with several lifetimes' experience doing this sort of thing.'

'Oh,' said Martha laughing. 'You mean like the last of the Time Lords?'

'Yeah, I think he'd do,' grinned the Doctor. 'If only we could find him.'

'I see,' said Captain Georgina. 'You can help us, can you?'

'Can you?' added Martha.

The Doctor met her eye. 'I'm working on it,' he said.

He continued to work on the transmat booth for hours. Archibald and Captain Georgina eventually left him to it and went back to the canapé-scoffing party. Martha felt torn between joining them and staying with the Doctor.

'You want anything to eat?' she said. He didn't even seem to hear her.

She made her way over to the human crew and badgers. They all seemed to be having fun, chatting, telling jokes and stories, and generally not giving a stuff about the problems facing them. Thomas made an unsubtle effort to impress Martha with a story about how fast he liked to drive. Archibald, grinning with new confidence, told the old joke about why pirates are called pirates. And Captain Georgina responded to this with a light and tinkling laugh. Martha smiled to herself. Was Archibald flirting? Was Captain Georgina? Did they even know themselves?

Only she and the Doctor seemed bothered that the ship might explode at any moment. Or maybe they were all just making the most of whatever time they had left. She felt glad for the three badgers, so clearly loving every minute of it. But she was also envious of them, and their ability to fit in. It wasn't just being from Earth that made her an outsider. Now she'd met the Doctor she couldn't just stand idle.

And that was when it struck her. They had a chance. Or at least, they had a choice. A choice between just waiting for the *Brilliant* to explode and daring to brave the pirates.

'Archie,' she said.

Archibald grinned at her. 'What you get,' he said, 'if you cross a robot with a pirate?'

'Never mind that now,' she told him. 'I need your help.'

'OK,' he said.

'What do you think the rest of your lot would make of the canapés?' she asked him.

'Huh,' he said. 'They'd like the cheese ones best.'

'What is it?' asked Captain Georgina. 'Have you thought of something we can do?' Around her, other people's conversations died down. The party had been a pretence; they were all desperate to escape.

'Yeah, I think so,' said Martha. 'I think we have a chance. If we can get out of the loop, we just need Archie, Joss and Dash to tell their friends what they found here. The food, the drink, a whole different way of living.'

'But they want the experimental drive!' said Thomas.

'No,' said Martha. 'Whoever's hiring them does. And while they do what they're told, the badgers are just slaves.'

'No one,' said Dashiel slowly, 'owns anyone.'

'Exactly!' said Martha. 'That's what you have to tell them!'

No one said anything. The badgers looked at one another, the humans watched with bated breath. And then Martha jumped at a voice that came from right behind her.

'I think that's brilliant,' said the Doctor.

'Yeah?' said Martha, swelling with pride.

'Oh yeah,' said the Doctor. 'Double A-star and probably a badge.'

'But will it work?' asked Captain Georgina.

'Oh,' said the Doctor, 'who knows? But you've got a choice between certain death and a small hope of surviving. You're a clever lady, you work out the maths.'

'And you can get us out of the loop?' she asked.

'Oh yeah,' said the Doctor. 'Easy. I just need to get down to the engine rooms and swap some stuff around. I've got some equipment down there which can help.'

'But how will you get there when the transmat isn't working?' asked Martha.

'Well, it's not working quite like it should be,' admitted the Doctor. 'But I've been talking to it. And I think we've reached an accommodation.'

'Doctor,' said Martha, carefully. 'You're not going to do anything dangerous, are you?'

'Of course I am,' he said.

'If anything goes wrong…' said Martha.

'Then we take the consequences,' he finished for her. 'That's how it works.'

'You can program the engines from here,' Captain Georgina told him.

'I already have done,' said the Doctor quickly. He seemed pleased to move on from Martha's concern for his safety. 'But I need the systems up here and the stuff down there to be doing slightly different things. That's how we jump-start the ship. It's quite clever, really.'

'So we're going down to the engine rooms?' asked Martha, already making her way over to the transmit booth.

'Er,' said the Doctor. 'I am,' he said. 'I kind of need you to stay here.'

'Oh,' said Martha. 'OK, whatever you want.'

'Really?' he said, surprised.

'Well it's going to be important, isn't it?' she asked.

'Oh yeah,' said the Doctor, a little too quickly. 'I need you to be up here watching.'

'Watching what?' she said, looking back at the horseshoe of computers. 'I don't know how these controls work.'

'Not the controls. I don't wholly trust the badgers. And I really don't trust the crew.' He grinned. 'I quite liked Mrs Wingsworth.'

But something in his eyes didn't feel quite right. She folded her arms. 'What?' she said.

'What?' he said back at her, feigning innocence.

'There's something, isn't there?' she said. 'You're going to tell me.'

'All right,' he sighed. 'The transmat might not be much fun. It's meant to be instantaneous but we know there's some kind of delay. And if I'm lucky I won't notice while I'm inside it...'

'But if you do?' asked Martha, her eyes wide in horror. She didn't know quite how a transmat worked but imagined him scrambled like the eggy material that still blocked the doorway.

'Oh, I'll pull together,' he said lightly. Before she could stop him he'd opened the door of the transmat, was inside and at the controls. 'Play nicely while I'm gone,' he said.

'But Doctor,' she said, tugging on the door which refused to open. 'I don't even know what you're going to do!'

'You know what?' said the Doctor. 'Neither do I.' He grinned. 'Ah well. Sure I'll think of something.' And with a pop he vanished from the booth.

TWELVE

It didn't hurt quite as much as he'd expected. Yes, it hurt a lot. And yes, a human being would never have survived. A transmat machine takes you apart and puts you back together again, but the whole thing is over so quickly you shouldn't even notice. This one had taken its time. The Doctor had felt himself being slowly reassembled, an agonising torture where there was not enough of him to scream. But as he emerged from the transmat booth into the dark, noisy engine rooms, he felt pretty much OK.

His legs buckled underneath him, and he fell face first onto the floor.

He struggled to get up again and found his limbs weren't quite responding. His arms and legs tingled with pins and needles, like they did when he regenerated. Perhaps that's what he'd done, his body responding automatically to being pulled apart. He struggled to reach a hand up to his face. His fingers prodded familiar skin, tight over prominent bones. He had the same thick hair and long, furry sideburns and, though his mouth tasted all peculiar, his teeth seemed to be the same shape they'd been before. So, he was still the same man for the moment. But it said a lot about what he'd just been through that he'd not been sure.

As feeling came back to him, he heard hesitant, shuffling footsteps. It took effort to sit up, but going slowly he managed it. A group of mouthless men in leather aprons and Bermuda shorts huddled a short distance from him, in the narrow alleyway between the huge, dark machines. One mouthless man gestured and pointed to the far end of the engine rooms. The Doctor looked, squinting to make sense of what he saw. A tall, skinny man in a fetching pinstriped suit was stepping into a wall of scrambled egg.

'Huh thuh,' said the Doctor, watching him vanish. He had meant to say, 'Is that really what my hair looks like from the back?'

He sat there, recovering and, after a while, the mouthless men brought him a mug of tea with a picture of a sheep on it. His hands shook as he held the mug, but with each sip he felt better and better. The engines around him filled his head with noise and his skin felt itchy with grime. Yet the dark and solid machinery seemed immaculate, the air rich with the stink of detergent; he just imagined the dirt.

'Thank you,' he said as the mouthless men helped him up on his feet. They let him walk unaided but kept close in case he fell. The Doctor made his way to the wall-mounted controls for the experimental drive. A small porthole let him look into the machine itself, and he gazed in on the eerie light. The light was just the same as that inside the TARDIS's central column. It swirled and murmured, restless and alive.

'OK,' said the Doctor, checking over the engine controls. He made a mental note of the readings and how they differed from those upstairs on the bridge. The trick was then to get the TARDIS to make up for the difference. That would, he hoped, break them from the loop. Adjusting dials and switching levers, he felt the old speed and dexterity returning to his fingers. His thoughts were starting to speed up, too.

He spun on his heel, surprising the mouthless men, and hurried down the alleyway between the large machines to where the TARDIS waited. It took a moment to find the key and then he was inside. As always, stepping over the threshold filled him with sudden ease. His head felt clearer, his body less sore.

The console still sparked and smoked from where the ship had crashed into the *Brilliant*. The Doctor hurried over, swatting away the smoke and working the various controls. Yes, he could see it clearly now. They'd crashed because the *Brilliant* sat just outside space and time. Like jumping onto a moving bus, only it turned out to be rushing towards you.

The gravitic anomaliser protested as he wound it round to eight. He keyed in the values of the *Brilliant*'s two different Kodicek readings, and fired up the TARDIS's temporal shields. The idea was that he could give the *Brilliant* a nudge at the right angle and the starship's own systems would do the rest. He wouldn't even need to use the TARDIS's own reality-warping talents.

And then a thought struck him. A brilliant one.

He hurried round the console, pulling up the floor grating to expose the thick black cables coiling underneath. A bit of sonic screwdriver action, and he'd separated one of the connections. Bits of what might have been scrambled egg dripped from the open ends of cable.

He hurried back out of the TARDIS, bringing the cable so that it spooled out behind him, still connected at one end to the machinery of the TARDIS. It took a bit of negotiating the cable through the alleyway between the *Brilliant*'s huge and noisy engines, like getting the flex from a vacuum cleaner to fit round chairs and tables. But he reached the controls of the experimental drives, and then just had to find something that he might connect the cable to. The control desk of the experimental drive had input ports, but none quite fitted.

'Ah,' said the Doctor. 'Should have thought of that.'

He looked quickly all around for something that might help, but he knew there was little he could do. And then one of the mouthless men came forward with what looked like a squeezy bottle of ketchup. The Doctor tried plugging the TARDIS cable into each of the different ports, and once he'd identified the best fit the mouthless man sealed it in with the jelly-like sealant that oozed from the squeezy bottle. It was the same fast-acting, impossibly strong stuff that had sealed the hole in the side of the ship when Archibald's capsule had torn through it.

'Well done you,' said the Doctor to the mouthless man as he tested the join was secure. In fact, the join was stronger than the cable was itself. The Doctor hurried back to the TARDIS.

A group of mouthless men huddled at the doorway, peering into the huge interior but not daring to venture any further.

'Well?' said the Doctor. 'Aren't you going to say how it's bigger on the inside?' The mouthless men turned to look at him. 'No, I guess not,' he said. 'Look, you can ride with me but it's going to be bumpy. Or you can stay here, which will probably be the same. Your choice.'

It was a little disappointing, but none of the mouthless men would come with him. He shrugged, ducked between them into the TARDIS and dashed over to the controls. The mouthless men watched him from the open doorway, the thick black cable snaking between their legs back to the controls of the experimental drive. He could see them wanting to ask him what he had just done. 'I've bolted your ship to mine,' he said. 'And now I can run your systems from here. But my ship can also compensate for some of the loopy stuff happening. So I might even be able to control aspects of the loop itself. And then we're laughing. Ha ha!'

The mouthless men nodded, though not as keenly as he'd have liked. Still, there was little he could do about that now.

'You probably want to stand back a bit,' he told them. They retreated in fear as he worked the controls in front of him. It had been a while since he'd last tried to take off with the doors still open, he thought. Probably because it was such a dangerous thing to do. Dangerous and reckless. Dangerous and reckless and irresponsible. Just his thing, really.

He released the TARDIS handbrake.

With the familiar low rasping, grating from deep within its own strange engines, the TARDIS began to warp the material of space-time around it. The Doctor stood resolute at the controls as what might have been a tornado tore through the open doors and sent papers, sweets and his 1966 Martin Rowlands trimphone whirling all around him. Where before the open TARDIS doors had looked out into the engine rooms, the way was now blocked by a wall of pulsing, straining scrambled egg. The tornado whirled ever faster round and round him, howling and shrieking in time to the noise of the TARDIS's engines.

And then it was suddenly over, the sweets and paper and designer telephone crashing to the floor.

'Said it was easy,' said the Doctor, though only to himself. And he bounded through the open, eggless TARDIS doors and back into the *Brilliant*'s engine rooms. 'Oh,' he said, stopping suddenly. 'I don't think that's quite right.'

Outside, the engine rooms lay silent. The huge machinery stood perfectly still. There was no one about.

'Hello?' called the Doctor. No one responded. 'I know you can't speak,' he called out. 'But maybe you could hit something, make some kind of noise.'

Again there was nothing but silence.

Moving slowly, warily, the Doctor followed the thick black cable from the TARDIS as it wended along the alleyway between the still machines. The cut-off end of the cable lay on the floor in front of where the controls for the experimental drive had been. It had been cut off with a knife.

'Ah,' said the Doctor. 'That shouldn't have happened.'

He examined the empty space, and it was clear the experimental drive had been torn from the housing in which it had been secured. For a moment, he wondered if perhaps realigning the *Brilliant* had made the drive implode, which would be quite a neat solution to everything. But in his hearts he knew that that couldn't have been what had happened.

The walls of the engine room were a mishmash of car-sized patches of red-jelly sealant. The Doctor could see that at least six or seven pirate capsules had torn their way aboard the ship and then torn their way off again. Any of the mouthless men who'd been in the engine rooms when the pirate ships tore through the hull would have been quickly sucked out into space.

'Ah,' said the Doctor. 'I must be running late again.'

Desperate to find out what had happened to Martha, he grabbed the cut-off end of the cable, and quickly gathered it back up into the TARDIS. He'd repair the link later, when he knew Martha was OK. Locking the door of the TARDIS, he made for the transmat booth. With the ship realigned it should be working properly once again.

He keyed the controls and nothing happened. Annoyed, he checked over the transmat systems. The booth he was in seemed to be in good working order, but it couldn't reach the booth upstairs.

A chill ran through the Doctor.

He dashed down the alleyway between the huge machines, to the door that he'd only ever seen before blocked by scrambled egg. There was no egg now, and he ran out into the plush-carpeted passageway. The wood-panelled walls were patched with more car-sized holes where pirate capsules had punched through.

He ran left, left again and then right, and took the stairs three at a time. Halfway up the staircase to the ballroom, he saw the first dead body.

A blue Balumin man lay sprawled at the top of the stairs, a terrible, blank expression on his face. Further into the ballroom lay two more blackened bodies.

The Doctor made his way into the cocktail lounge, expecting to see more dead. But the cocktail lounge was empty, the whole bay window that looked out onto the Ogidi Galaxy now a great long patch of jelly sealant. Most of the Balumin would have died in space, the pirates had shot the rest.

Upstairs, the walls were likewise patched with red jelly sealant. The Doctor made his way along the crew's small quarters and through to the door to the bridge. There was no wall of scrambled egg blocking his way, and he stepped through quickly. The horseshoe of computers had been smashed apart. And in the gap lay the dead body of Captain Georgina Wet-Eleven of the Second Mid Dynasty.

There were a few other corpses around, but there was nothing to be done for them now. Instead, the Doctor moved quickly past them to examine the sparking remains of the computers, but they could tell him nothing. He had no idea how long it had been since the loop had come apart, nor where the pirate ship had got to now. He had lost Martha to them again. But, as he'd promised himself before, he would do whatever it took to find her.

He rummaged in the pockets of his suit jacket for a bit of paper and a pen, and almost cut himself on the dagger he'd confiscated from the unconscious Dashiel all that time ago. When they'd still been enemies and people couldn't die.

'Doctor?'

He spun round on the heel of his trainer. The egg-shaped, orange and tentacled Mrs Wingsworth stood in the doorway of the bridge. She no longer had any of her extravagant jewellery and her flimsy dress had been spattered with muck and blood.

'Hi,' said the Doctor.

'Whatever are you doing, dear?' she asked.

'Writing a note in case there were any survivors,' he said. He left the note on the wreck of the horseshoe of computers and hurried over to her. 'Are you all right?' he asked.

'Oh, we soldier on, dear,' she said. 'But you know there's nothing to drink downstairs.'

'Shocking,' he said. 'I'd complain.'

'I did!' said Mrs Wingsworth, laughing. 'Only there's no one here to take the slightest bit of notice!' The laugh died in her throat, but the Doctor could see her refusing to let him see how scared she'd been, how much she'd suffered.

'It's going to be all right,' he said. 'I promise you.'

Mrs Wingsworth reached out her tentacles to him. 'Martha!' she said, a tremor in her voice. 'She said I had to find you!'

'And you have,' said the Doctor kindly. 'It's going to be all right. I'm here now. You just have to tell me what I missed.'

Mrs Wingsworth, tears streaming down her egg-shaped orange body, did her best to explain.

'The pirates,' she said. 'They came. They killed *everybody*. And no one's coming back.'

THIRTEEN

'**Y**ou know what?' said the Doctor, stood in the transmat booth. 'Neither do I.' He grinned. 'Ah well. Sure I'll think of something.' And with a pop he vanished.

Martha sighed. There was nothing to do but wait until he'd sorted everything out. She turned to join the party of humans and three badgers. And then she froze.

Projected on the wall, the spiky peach of the badger pirates' spaceship had begun to move. Tiny pirate capsules spewed from the back of the ship, each zipping round to attack the *Brilliant* head on. They fired their weapons, and another screen to the left blared warning signals about the *Brilliant*'s shields.

Captain Georgina, Thomas and some of the other crew were racing to the horseshoe of computers. 'Get a channel open!' Captain Georgina shouted. 'Get a channel open!'

'Open, sir,' said Thomas quickly, busy at the controls.

'Archie!' said Captain Georgina. 'Time for you to do your stuff.'

'Oh, er, yeah,' said Archibald, hurrying to join the human crew. 'Uh, Captain Florence?' he said, and Martha could see how awkward and scared he was about just speaking to the air. 'This is, uh, Archie. There's food 'ere. Good food.'

Thomas fussed with the controls, getting only static in response. And then a voice was heard loud and clear. 'Archie?' said a vicious-sounding badger woman. 'You're in *big* trouble, y'swab!'

For a moment they stared at Archibald, who could only shrug. Then something smashed into the *Brilliant* and the impact knocked them all off their feet.

'Keep trying!' shouted Captain Georgina as she scrambled back to the controls. 'You've got to convince them!'

'Yeah,' said Archie. Dashiel and Jocelyn, holding hands, joined him at the horseshoe of computers and they all tried appealing to their former comrades.

Captain Georgina signalled the rest of the human crew. 'We're going to have boarders,' she told them. 'You'll take your positions and hold them from the engine rooms.'

'Sir,' said the brunette. 'The Doctor took our guns.' It was true: a mess of broken weapons lay littered on the floor, their innards used to build an almost working Teasmade.

'Hell,' said Captain Georgina. She shoved Archibald

aside and took his place next to Thomas. 'This is Captain Georgina Wet-Eleven of the Starship *Brilliant*,' she told the attacking badgers. 'You are in violation of intergalactic transit codes six, fourteen and twenty. You will desist your attack *at once*, or we will blast you from the sky.'

There was a pause, and just for a moment Martha thought the defiance in the captain's tone might have made the pirates reconsider.

'Ha!' said the gruff female voice they'd heard before. 'Bring it on!'

Again they were thrown from their feet as something smashed into the ship. And again. 'They're 'ere!' said Jocelyn, from the ground beside Martha.

'S'OK,' said Dashiel. 'We'll tell 'em.' He led Jocelyn quickly out of the bridge, through the door which was no longer blocked by scrambled egg. They passed a flustered Mrs Wingsworth as they went.

'Get that passenger out of here!' shouted Captain Georgina. A couple of the human crew ran to bustle Mrs Wingsworth off the bridge, but Martha hurried over.

'She's with me,' she said. Again the ship buckled as something smashed into it. The human crew obviously decided that they had better things to do than worry about the passengers. Martha led Mrs Wingsworth out into the crew's quarters, away from all the panic.

'More haste, less speed, I always say, dear,' Mrs Wingsworth said, rolling her eyes. 'What *has* been going on?'

'The Doctor let us out of the time loop,' Martha explained. 'But now the pirates are attacking.'

'What, like those three dears?' said Mrs Wingsworth.

'Remember what they were like when they first got here?' said Martha.

Before Mrs Wingsworth could reply, the wall exploded just ahead of them. Martha barely registered the Smart car-sized capsule that had crashed aboard before she was lifted off her feet. A capsule-sized gash in the side of the ship gaped out onto open space. Martha tried to scream but the air was being sucked out into space just as she was. She flailed her arms and legs as she fell towards the hole, but there was nothing to grab on to. . .

Something yanked her ankle hard and this time she managed to cry out. Twisting back, she found Mrs Wingsworth clutching her with one tentacle, the other gripping round the bunk of one of the human crew's beds. They both hung in mid air, Mrs Wingsworth's tentacles taut and skinny with the strain. Her glittering, golden jewellery buckled and broke, each piece dancing in the air as it tumbled into space.

'Oh really!' muttered Mrs Wingsworth, her teeth clenched as she fought to keep her grip. 'That used to be my mother's.'

Martha struggled for breath as the hole in the side of the ship tried to swallow her. A human crewmember – the pretty brunette – tried to reach for Martha's hand. They brushed fingers, didn't quite catch hold, and then the brunette tumbled out into the dark, starry vacuum.

As she fell out, she was hit by flecks of the red, jelly-like substance fast sealing the hole behind her.

Martha and Mrs Wingsworth crashed down onto the hard floor the moment the hole had been sealed. They lay there panting, then Mrs Wingsworth grabbed Martha's ankle again and dragged her into the small room with the bed in it she'd clung to. She slammed the small door just at the same time as another capsule burst through the far wall. Martha hugged her tight as, beyond the closed door, they heard the screams of yet more human crewmembers being sucked out into space.

The *Brilliant* lurched again and again as the pirate capsules smashed into it. Martha felt sick and terrified. But it seemed to be quiet now, on the far side of the door. She put her ear to the door, and heard muffled shouts and shooting. The badger pirates were pillaging the ship.

She desperately needed to know where the Doctor had got to. He wouldn't leave them to die like this. She knew he'd come for her somehow.

'You can't go out there, dear!' squealed Mrs Wingsworth. Martha hadn't even been aware of her hands working to unlock the door.

'I've got to find the Doctor,' she said.

'No you don't!' insisted Mrs Wingsworth, and swiped Martha away from the door with a tentacle like a tree trunk. 'You're not going to do anything silly. We both have to—'

The door disintegrated in a sudden ball of pink light.

Had Martha still been in front of it, she would have been obliterated herself. Mrs Wingsworth whimpered as a helmeted badger pirate stormed into the small room, prodding her with his gun.

'You Marfa?' the badger said bluntly, with a gruff female voice.

'Er,' said Mrs Wingsworth. 'I might be, dear.'

The badger pirate raised his gun at her. 'No wait!' cried Martha from where she lay on the floor. 'I'm Martha. Just leave this one alone.'

'Huh,' said the badger pirate. She reached down, grabbed Martha's arm in her hairy paw and started dragging her out into the passageway.

'Now really!' Mrs Wingsworth began to protest.

'Please!' Martha told her as she was taken roughly away. 'Stay there, stay safe. You have to find the Doctor!' And then she was round the side of one of the capsules and could not see Mrs Wingsworth any more.

The badger pirate dragged her back onto the *Brilliant*'s bridge. A whole gang of badger pirates awaited them, the last three of the human crew kneeling in front of them, their hands clasped to their heads. Thomas, Captain Georgina and a pretty, red-haired girl were all that had survived. The rest, Martha realised, must have been shot or sucked out into space. With these last three survivors were Archibald, Jocelyn and Dashiel. A male badger was shouting at them, brandishing a bent silver tray.

'But Stanley,' Dashiel tried to explain. 'It happened. We ate the food and then it was there again!'

Stanley was about to say something when he saw Martha being brought in. 'Good one, Zuzia,' he told the badger gripping Martha's arm. 'Put her with the rest.'

'But she's good,' said Archibald quietly.

'Shaddap!' snapped Stanley. Zuzia led Martha over to the three human crew, and gestured with her gun for Martha to kneel in the same way that they did. Martha did as she was bidden, taking her place between Captain Georgina and Thomas. Blood dripped from Thomas's handlebar moustache and he wouldn't meet her eye.

'You don't have to hurt us,' said Martha calmly.

'Nah,' said Stanley, coming over. 'But we wanta.' To prove his point, he cuffed Thomas across the face with the back of his paw. He leered at Martha, his breath hot and stinky in her face. But before he could hit her or hurt her, another badger came running in.

'Yeah, Toby?' said Stanley.

'We got the drive,' said the newcomer.

'Hah!' said Stanley. 'Get it back to the captain. We just gotta finish up 'ere.'

'Aw,' said Toby. 'Can I watch?'

'Get off!' snapped Stanley. 'S'more important.'

'Right,' said Toby, and he hurried away. Stanley turned back to his prisoners.

'Don't do this,' Martha told him.

'I got orders, ain't I?' said Stanley.

'Yeah, but no one owns anyone.' said Dashiel.

'Hah!' laughed Stanley. But there was a murmur from some of the other badgers. Martha dared to glance round at them. No, she could see they weren't happy with three of their prisoners being badgers from their own ship. 'You reckon?' Stanley leered at Dashiel.

'Yeah,' said Dashiel, daring to get to his feet. The other pirates still kept their guns on him. 'We don't 'ave to be slaves alla time.'

Stanley snorted at him, but clearly had no answer to this. He wrinkled his wet, black badger nose, and Martha could see him thinking this proposition over. Then, without any fuss, he raised his gun and shot Dashiel squarely in the chest. Dashiel screamed as the pink light engulfed him.

'Dash!' cried Jocelyn, but before she could move, Archibald had grabbed her, stopping her from getting shot herself.

The pink light died away and Dashiel's dead body toppled over onto the floor.

'Hah,' said Stanley.

'Tha's *bad*, Stanley,' said Archibald, hugging Jocelyn as she sobbed into his shoulder.

'Yeah?' said Stanley. 'Captain Florence ain't 'appy wiv 'im. You flew off before you was told.' So, thought Martha, that explained why only the three badger pirates had got aboard the *Brilliant* at first. Dashiel hadn't been able to wait.

'Dash said we'd get the spoils,' said Archibald quietly.

'I know that!' said Stanley. 'He's a cheater. We all 'ave to wait till she says we can go. Uvverwise it ain't fair.'

'Yeah,' said Archibald. 'But…'

'No but!' snapped Stanley. 'Captain Florence wants ta see you and Joss. Tell you off 'erself.' Martha saw Archibald and Jocelyn both shiver with terror at the thought of whatever punishment their captain might have in store for them. 'And you can take 'er that one, too,' added Stanley, waggling his gun in the direction of Martha.

'Me?' she said, horrified. 'Why me?'

'Archie's been tellin' us all about ya,' said Stanley. 'You put stuff in his 'ead.'

'What, the canapés?' she said, trying to sound surprised and innocent. 'That's just a bit of food.'

'Yeah!' nodded Stanley. 'An' now look what 'e's like!'

Martha looked over at Archibald. He grinned and waved at her. Then seemed to remember where he was, and put his paws slowly back on the top of his head.

'See?' said Stanley. He waved his gun at the rest of the prisoners, teasing them as to who he'd kill next. Then he shrugged. 'Get 'em up.'

The other badgers came forward and the prisoners – Martha, the human crew, Archibald and Jocelyn – got slowly to their feet. The three other humans were bruised and bloody where they'd been knocked about. Captain Georgina still looked like she'd been modelling for some glossy magazine, though. She stood taller than the badgers, and the look in her eye showed she would not be intimidated.

'Take your own lot,' she said. 'But you'll leave Martha here with me.'

'Yeah?' said Stanley. 'But you're all gonna die, ain't ya?' He turned and shot at the horseshoe of computers, which exploded in pink flame.

'No!' shouted Captain Georgina and, ignoring the other badgers and their guns, ran over to the blazing, bright pink bonfire that had once been her command. When she turned to face the badgers again, her eyes were terrible to see. Stanley grinned at her, like she'd just given him permission to kill her.

'Captain,' said Martha carefully. 'You should come back over here. You're still a prisoner. Stanley will show you mercy.'

'Hah!' said Stanley. 'Mercy!' He raised his gun.

'You're not going to get away with this,' said Captain Georgina with majestic calm.

'Yeah I am,' said Stanley, and he shot her. Captain Georgina didn't cry out as the pink light engulfed her. Martha, horrified, thought she might even have provoked her own death, rather than be taken prisoner. Everyone else seemed utterly terrified of what might happen to them at the hands of Captain Florence.

'Right,' said Stanley. And he led the badgers and their prisoners off the bridge and back to their capsules. Martha was forced into the back of one capsule, squeezed in between Stanley and another badger called Kitty Rose. It was like being in the back of her brother's car, her knees up by her elbows and no room to even breathe. Through the window, she saw Archibald being squashed into the back of another capsule further along the passageway, and Jocelyn escorted to another.

Thomas and the pretty, red-haired girl remained standing in the passageway, looking unsure what to do.

'You're not taking them with us?' asked Martha as the capsule door closed.

In front of her, Stanley checked the readings on the dashboard in front of him, checking that all the other pirate capsules were ready to go. 'Nah,' he said. A thought struck him, and he leaned round in his seat to leer at her again. 'Gonna show 'em mercy.'

He stabbed a button on the controls in front of him with his hairy paw. The capsule lurched backwards, smashing out of the side of the *Brilliant* and out into the vacuum of space. Martha smacked her head on the back of the capsule, and as she recovered herself saw the starship falling away from her, a weird steel sailing ship with glittering solar sails. Its hull was blotchy with red patches where the badgers' capsules had torn through it. Martha watched the other capsules tearing out from the *Brilliant*. From the hole her own capsule had just made, she saw Thomas and the red-haired girl, clutching each other tightly as they tumbled into space.

Stanley and the other badger, Kitty Rose, worked the simple controls, and the capsule turned slowly round to face the spiky peach of the pirate ship. Stanley dum-de-dummed as they made their way forward. When she'd seen it on the screens aboard the *Brilliant*, Martha had had no idea of the scale of the pirate ship, but it was enormous. The spikes weren't guns but narrow tower blocks, each one the size of the hospital she used to work in. She realised there must be thousands and thousands of badgers aboard. It was less a ship than a moving city.

Still humming to himself contentedly, Stanley steered them round into the vast hangar at the back of the ship where thousands of identical capsules sat waiting. They parked in a free space about a mile into the hangar, and Stanley patted his thighs in time to his humming while he waited for a signal from the controls on his dashboard to say it was OK to get out.

Martha prised herself out of the cramped back seat, her knees and elbows aching. Stanley shrugged at her discomfort. The other badgers emerged from capsules across the way, prodding Archibald and Jocelyn forwards with their guns. Archibald grinned at Martha like this was all a game.

'You can see where I got made,' he told her.

'Nah,' said Stanley. 'You got uvver stuff to do.'

Their captors led them to what was almost a golf-car, which whined and whispered as it took them to the end of the huge hangar and dropped them off at a lift. Stanley hummed again as they waited for the lift to arrive. One of the other badgers recognised the tune and dared to join in the humming. Stanley glared at him and he quickly stopped.

The spacious lift seemed to go sideways as well as up and down, and Martha tried to make sense of the complex instructions Stanley gave it. She was still sure she'd be able to escape somehow.

They stood in awkward silence as the lift rushed them upwards and along. Stanley and the other badgers seemed to itch with excitement about wherever they were going. Whatever Captain Florence had in store for her prisoners, it would, Martha realised, be entertainment for the other badger pirates.

Eventually the lift came to a stop, and the doors slid open with a ding. Sweet and spicy air wafted in to them, a mix of pot-pourri and curry. Stanley beckoned his prisoners forward, and Martha stepped out into a passageway of hanging silks and incense. Not at all what she'd expected on any kind of spaceship.

As she proceeded down the corridor of pungent, hanging silks, Martha glimpsed a frenzy of activity going on out of view. The silks hid badgers in various loose-fitting, sweaty clothes as they busied themselves at banks of complex controls. They were, realised Martha, on the bridge of the pirate ship. But the captain here had tried to make it look homely.

At the end of the passageway, a great viewing gallery looked out into space. Looking up and at an angle, Martha could see the Starship *Brilliant*. She could never get used to space being in three dimensions. In front of the window, silhouetted by the stars, stood the dread Captain Florence.

'Captain!' said Stanley, hurrying over. He hung his head and his whole body bowed to her. 'I done as you asked,' he simpered. 'An' I brought you prisoners.'

Captain Florence slapped him so hard across the face

he skidded over the floor.

'Speak,' she said, her voice rich and husky, 'when yar spoken to, me hearty!'

She turned to see the prisoners she'd been brought. Martha gasped as the captain stepped into the light. Captain Florence stood taller than any of her pirates. She wore a loose, collarless blouse. Her bare, bristly arms were taut and muscular, like she spent her whole time working out. A jagged scar worked across her forehead, dipped behind an eyepatch, and then continued down her hairy cheek.

'Er,' said Martha. 'It's very nice to meet you.'

Captain Florence looked her slowly up and down, like a butcher might appraise a fatted calf. Then she clicked her paws, called out 'Dylan!' to one of the badgers working behind the hanging silks, and turned back to watch the *Brilliant*, perfectly framed in the middle of the great bay window.

'Um,' said Martha, as badgers – one of them called Dylan – ran about behind her, doing whatever they'd just been bidden. She heard paws working on keyboards and levers being pressed.

And then a brilliant white beam of light struck out from underneath them and blew the *Brilliant* to smithereens.

FOURTEEN

The pirate ship *Mandelbrot Sett* had space for one million of the capsules it used for raiding other spacecraft. The hangar had a hundred levels, and each level divided into a grid of parking spaces, one hundred by one hundred.

This did not mean that there were capsules to fill all the parking spaces. The badgers expected to lose at least a few on any given raid, and over the years they'd taken part in several thousand raids. Though they replaced the capsules when they could, there were still various parking spaces dotted around the hangar's hundred floors.

And into one of these, with a rasping, grating sound as if the very fabric of space and time was being torn through, materialised the TARDIS.

The door of the TARDIS creaked open, and out stepped Mrs Wingsworth. 'Oh honestly, dear,' she said. 'It's like something died in here.'

The Doctor followed her out, sniffing at the air. 'Well that's car parks for you,' he said. 'Although, given where we are, it's likely something did.'

'Hoi!' shouted a gruff voice from behind the rows of parked pirate capsules. Two badger pirates came running forward, their guns at the ready. The Doctor turned to Mrs Wingsworth and winked. He had the first stirrings of a plan.

'Hullo!' he said to the two badgers cheerily. 'I'm the Doctor, this is Mrs Wingsworth. We've got an appointment with your captain.'

The two badgers skidded to a halt and looked nervously at one another. 'You gotta what?' one of them asked the Doctor.

'An appointment,' he said. 'Brought it from the *Brilliant* for her. She'll be livid if she doesn't get it.'

The badgers whispered to one another, obviously terrified of what would happen if they upset Captain Florence. And, he could see them thinking, no one would really be stupid enough to go see the captain if they didn't have to. 'OK,' said one of them. 'You come with us.'

'It'd be our pleasure,' said the Doctor. 'Wouldn't it, Mrs Wingsworth?'

'Certainly, dear,' she said. She hung her tentacle through the Doctor's proffered elbow, and they followed the two badgers as if they were on a night out at the opera.

'I'm sorry,' said the Doctor as they made their way

between the hundreds of pirate capsules towards the lift. 'I didn't catch your names.'

'Karl,' said one of the badgers. 'Tha's Robbie. We're on duty.'

'And you're very professional about it,' said the Doctor. 'I'll be telling your captain how impressed we are with you.'

Karl and Robbie grinned at each other and quickened their pace towards the lifts. The lift itself, when it came, was big enough to fit two or three of the pirate capsules into, which was probably useful for getting things repaired, thought the Doctor. Before stepping inside, he turned to the two badgers.

'Well,' he said. 'You two have been extremely kind. Mrs Wingsworth and I are both very touched.'

'It's been simply splendid!' agreed Mrs Wingsworth, perhaps enjoying the act a little bit too much.

'But we mustn't detain you any longer,' said the Doctor. 'You must get back to your duties.'

'Uh,' said Robbie. 'We, uh, don't come wiv ya?'

'Oh no!' said the Doctor appalled at the very idea. 'You're on duty! What would your captain say?'

The two badgers stepped quickly back from the lift, and the Doctor worked the controls. The lift went up and down and could also go sideways, and it took the Doctor almost two whole seconds to work out how to get them to the bridge. He keyed in the instructions and, with a ding, the lift doors began to close. Mrs Wingsworth waved politely to Karl and Robbie.

When the lift doors had closed and the lift was on its way, Mrs Wingsworth let out a long sigh. 'Well!' she said. 'I never thought we'd get away with it.'

'Oh, it's easy enough,' said the Doctor. 'I do this all the time.'

'What, just walking onto alien pirate spaceships as if you own the place?' laughed Mrs Wingsworth.

'Oh yeah,' said the Doctor. 'It's like a hobby.'

Mrs Wingsworth laughed. And then the laugh tailed off and became more like she was choking. The Doctor realised she was forcing herself not to cry.

'Sorry,' said the Doctor. 'Forgot how this sort of thing can take a bit of getting used to.'

'Oh no!' wailed Mrs Wingsworth. 'It's been amazing, dear! I've never felt more alive. The first time they killed me, I was absolutely terrified. But it didn't matter after that. And I watched your friend Martha. She didn't have a gun like they did, and she stood up to them! She used her brains. Tried to get that Archibald one drunk!'

The Doctor laughed. 'One-track mind, that one,' he said. 'You can tell she's from London.'

'You don't understand!' said Mrs Wingsworth, desperately. 'I've never... We never... I've never stood up to anyone before.' She hung her head, sadly, like how could he even look at her now?

'Ah,' said the Doctor. 'You've got a big family, haven't you, Mrs Wingsworth?'

She looked up at him, surprised. 'Whatever's that got to do with anything, dear?' she said.

'You talk about them all the time,' he told her. 'Your cousin who did this, your uncle who did that.'

'There's nothing wrong with being proud of your lineage,' she said.

'But you never tell stories about things you've done yourself,' he said.

'Oh,' she said. 'Well.' She shuffled awkwardly, stroking her tentacles together. 'I suppose that's because I don't have very much to tell you.'

The Doctor smiled at her. 'I guess not,' he said. 'There's not really anything exciting in how you stood up to the pirates. Or how you got killed once or twice. Or teaching Dashiel how to say "please" and "thank you".'

Mrs Wingsworth shivered. 'They killed him,' she said. 'I saw his body.'

'I'm sorry,' said the Doctor, kindly.

'If I hadn't won him over…' said Mrs Wingsworth.

'He'd have been a poorer badger,' the Doctor finished for her. 'You showed him a better life. And that's what he died for.'

Mrs Wingsworth sniffed. 'I suppose.'

'So,' said the Doctor. 'You've got stories to tell your clever family when I get you back to them.'

'Oh,' she said. 'I don't expect they'll be very interested, dear. They never were in me. That's why I was on the *Brilliant*. You see,' she added nervously, 'it wasn't the war I was running away from.'

The Doctor took one of her tentacles in his hands, calming her. 'You should be proud of all you've done here,' he said.

'Oh, I am!' she said, snatching her tentacle from him. 'It's just they would never think so. Because they never do!' Her eyes opened wide at this sudden revelation. 'Because,' she said, more quietly, 'they just aren't worth the bother.'

'You don't pick your family,' said the Doctor. 'Trust me, it's an achievement just to survive them sometimes.'

Mrs Wingsworth laughed, a deep belly rumble rather than the high, sarcastic tinkling she had used before, when laughing at other people's failings. 'All right,' she said, slapping a tentacle against the Doctor's shoulder in a manner most unseemly for a Balumin of her age. 'No more feeling sorry for myself and sulking in the corner. And they can either like it or lump it.'

'You go, girl,' said the Doctor.

'Believe me, Doctor, I intend to,' said Mrs Wingsworth. 'Now let's sort out this wretched pirate captain, shall we?'

And with a ding the lift arrived at the bridge of the pirate ship. The doors eased open to reveal a passageway of hanging silks, behind which badgers worked controls. The air was rich with exotic spices, flavours from all over the cosmos. It was a sign of just how widely travelled these badger pirates were. Mrs Wingsworth took the Doctor's elbow, and – again acting as if they were honoured guests – they stepped forward. At the end of the passageway, they could see Archibald and Jocelyn held captive by their former badger comrades.

And, down some steps, Martha and the ferocious pirate captain gazed out of a wide bay window at the Starship *Brilliant*.

The Doctor and Mrs Wingsworth were just in time to see a beam of blinding light strike the *Brilliant* and blast it into pieces.

'No!' yelled Martha at the pirate captain. 'You've killed the Doctor!'

'Er,' said the Doctor. 'Actually, she missed.' The badgers wheeled round, astonished at this intrusion. 'Sorry to butt in,' said the Doctor, skipping down the steps to join them in front of the great bay window. He waved at Archibald and Jocelyn and winked at Martha. 'But we saw a light on and thought we'd just pop in. Any danger of a cup of tea? Or some of those cheese and pineapple on sticks?'

'I said!' said Archibald, straining from the badger who held him captive to tell his other former comrades. 'I said they was good!'

'You all right?' the Doctor asked Martha.

'Yeah,' she said. 'Fine. Getting a bit bored of all this, to be honest.'

'Oh dear,' said the Doctor. 'Well, don't worry. Have it all fixed in a jiffy.' He turned to the tall badger captain in the collarless blouse and eyepatch. She was tall for one of the badgers, her high-heeled boots meaning she could look the Doctor straight in the eye. 'Hello there!' he said. 'You must be Captain Florence. Nice to meet—'

Captain Florence roared, and the next thing the Doctor

knew he was skidding on his back across the floor, the impression of a hairy fist hot across his face. 'Ow,' he said. Beside him lay another badger pirate, who'd clearly just suffered a similar rebuke from the captain.

'Now really,' muttered Mrs Wingsworth from where she stood by Martha. 'There's no need for that sort of behaviour.'

Captain Florence slapped her hard across the face. Mrs Wingsworth cowered under the blow, her tentacles raised to protect herself from being hit again.

'This ain't fun and games!' the captain roared. She looked up at the badgers who had emerged from the silk hangings so as not to miss seeing the fighting. 'Amelia!' she barked. 'Samuel! Find out how these two got aboard!' Two badger pirates scurried back to their controls.

The Doctor slowly picked himself up off the floor. 'There's really no need to be like this,' he said. 'I just wanted a chat.'

'You got sum'fin to offer us, 'ave ya?' leered Captain Florence.

'A better life than you've got at the moment,' said Mrs Wingsworth.

'With canapés and tea,' added Archibald. He turned to the badgers holding him and Jocelyn prisoner. 'You gotta try 'em,' he said. 'They're good.'

'Er, yeah,' said the Doctor. He stepped up to Captain Florence, though just out of reach of her punching him again. 'I'm disappointed you've not already listened to your friend Archie.'

Archibald bowed his head. 'I tried tellin' 'em,' he said.

'Oh, I'm not blaming you, Archie,' said the Doctor kindly. 'It's just a shame your management aren't open to suggestions. Not looking to new investment opportunities, to expand the business portfolio. Doesn't say much for their long-term prospects, if you ask me.'

Captain Florence pulled the gun from the belt around her waist. The Doctor tutted at her. 'Oh yes,' he said. 'That's the solution to everything, isn't it?'

But the captain didn't shoot him. Instead she shot Mrs Wingsworth. She didn't scream or cry out and, as the pink light ate her up, she kept staring defiantly at the captain. Captain Florence stepped back as the corpse collapsed in front of her. She looked a little shaken.

'Right,' she said, pointing the gun now at Martha.

'Captain!' called one of the badgers from behind the hanging silks. 'Karl and Robbie 'ave got the capsule what them two just arrived in!'

'Good,' said Captain Florence. 'Dump it inna space an' use it for target practice!'

The badgers cheered – target practice was clearly a bit of a treat. The Doctor felt his hearts heave. He couldn't believe their guns could destroy the TARDIS, but he didn't like the idea of her being sent tumbling off through space without him.

'Right,' said Captain Florence. 'Archie. You better tell us wha's so good 'bout this canner-pea stuff.'

Archibald wrenched free of the badgers holding him captive and came forward. He grinned at the Doctor and Martha, then turned on his heel, his back to Captain Florence. Instead, he addressed his former comrades.

'Yeah,' he said. 'They 'ad this food on the *Brillian*',' he told them. 'It was small but there was lots. And when you ate it all, then you jus' closed your eyes and there was more. It was good. It was food an' it was good to eat. It had… flavours. Tha's it, really.'

'Very eloquent,' said the Doctor. 'Very stirring. You should go into politics or something.'

'Yeah,' said Archie. He turned round to face Captain Florence and, perhaps because the Doctor and Martha were there, perhaps just because he'd been shown a better life, he didn't look at all fearful of her. 'It's good,' he told her.

'It may be,' she said to him quietly, and it looked like she had really considered what he'd said. 'But there's a problem, in't there?'

Behind her, through the bay window, the tiny shape of the TARDIS tumbled helplessly through space. Beams of blinding white light struck out at it from the pirate ship.

'What problem?' said Archibald.

'We blown up the *Brilliant*,' said Captain Florence. 'So there ain't no more good food for ya!'

'Oh yeah,' shrugged Archibald. He turned to the Doctor, and looked about to say something. But instead he screamed out as pink light engulfed him.

Captain Florence had shot him in the back.

FIFTEEN

Martha felt numb with horror as Archibald's body collapsed to the floor. She ran to the Doctor, who stretched his arms around her and held her tight.

'It's all right,' he said. 'I promise it's going to be all right.'

'Yeah,' growled Captain Florence savagely. 'But not fer you!'

The Doctor let Martha go and carefully ushered her round so that he stood between her and the captain. Martha glanced round looking for anything that might help them, but their only possible ally, Jocelyn, was being guarded by two other badger pirates.

'Yeah, OK,' the Doctor said to Captain Florence. 'I was just being optimistic. But that's not a bad thing, you know. And anyway. You think *we're* in trouble. What are your clients gonna do when they find out you blew up the *Brilliant*?'

Captain Florence laughed. 'We got the experimen'al

drive,' she said.

'No,' said the Doctor. 'You've taken the control desk for it. But the drive is a huge great engine at the heart of the ship. Which you've just blown up. Like nicking the remote control, but not the remote-control car. Schoolboy error.'

Martha didn't know if the Doctor was just bluffing – but neither did the badger pirates. The badgers around them, watching from the shadows and from behind the hanging silks, all began to murmur nervously. Captain Florence roared at them. There was a sudden, terrified silence. But Martha could tell that the Doctor had done what he always did, and undermined the tyrant. The badgers who had grown up on this miserable, vicious ship, were now just starting to question if there wasn't more to life.

'The client,' said Captain Florence. 'Said to nick the drive or blow up the ship. An' we done both.'

'Oh yeah,' said the Doctor, loud enough for everyone to hear him. 'I'm sure they'll see it that way. Might even deign to let you live.'

'What?' growled the captain.

'Well, look at it their way,' said the Doctor. 'There's this war coming. They want this experimental drive to use as a secret weapon. And they hire you lot to snatch it.'

'Yeah,' said Captain Florence.

'You're paid for your services. And very well you've gone about providing them. But what happens when you deliver this top secret experimental drive to them? You're then free to go to their rivals and, for a suitable fee, tell them what you stole.'

'Yeah,' said Captain Florence, her crafty little eyes lighting up at this suggestion.

'Exactly,' smiled the Doctor. 'So you think they're going to let you walk away?'

'What you mean?' asked Captain Florence. 'They're 'on'rable men, our clients.'

'So honourable they hired pirates to do their dirty work!' said Martha. Captain Florence leered at her.

'We're not pirates,' she said. 'We're independent financial wotsits.'

'You mean you're venture capitalists?' said the Doctor.

'Yeah,' said Captain Florence.

'Entrepreneurs?' asked Martha.

'Yeah,' said Captain Florence.

'Saps?' suggested the Doctor.

'Huh?' said Captain Florence.

'You're saps, stooges and patsies,' said the Doctor. 'They've got you doing their dirty work and you think that they'll be grateful!'

'Don't you get it?' added Martha. 'They hired you *because* you're nothing to them. Nothing at all. You've been taken for a ride.'

Stanley, the badger who'd brought Martha aboard and who still lay on the floor in the corner where Captain Florence had hit him, sat up. 'Does that mean,' he said, 'we won't get paid?'

'I assume you got half in advance,' said the Doctor. 'It might be better just to cut your losses and run.'

'Nah,' said Captain Florence.

'Nah, you're not going to run?' asked the Doctor. 'Or nah, you didn't get any money in advance? No don't tell me, I think I already know.'

Captain Florence didn't say anything. Instead she charged at him. The Doctor ducked under her, caught her hairy arm and tossed her lightly over his shoulder. She crashed into the floor, her high-heeled boot smacking into Stanley where he lay.

'Temper, temper,' said the Doctor.

Badgers rushed from behind the hanging silks, but they did not come to apprehend the Doctor. Instead, they gathered in a circle around the Doctor and the captain, all eager to see the fight. It was, thought Martha, like the fights that boys used to have at school. She hurried over to Jocelyn, their only other ally. Jocelyn's captors seemed to have forgotten her in the excitement.

Captain Florence got to her feet. She reached for the gun at her belt but it had gone. She looked up to see the Doctor holding it, as if he were surprised to find it in his hands.

'Oops,' he said.

'You gonna shoot me?' asked Captain Florence defiantly.

'Nah,' said the Doctor. 'You've got to have some other way for resolving disputes like this. Haven't you?'

Martha suspected that the badgers did just sort out their arguments by shooting one another.

'We duel,' said Captain Florence. She slid a short, jagged dagger from her belt. 'Can you duel?'

'I expect so,' said the Doctor. And to Martha's amazement he withdrew a matching dagger from the pocket of his suit jacket. 'Took this from Dashiel earlier,' he said. 'Think it's what he would have wanted.' He handed the captain's gun to one of the other badgers.

Captain Florence lunged at him with her dagger. The Doctor dodged, light on his feet like a well-practised wrestler. Captain Florence lunged again, and again she missed.

'Martha,' said the Doctor, enjoying himself but never for an instant taking his eyes off the captain. 'Did I ever take you back to Roman-era Egypt?'

'Er,' said Martha. 'Don't think so.'

'Well,' said the Doctor, dancing nimbly around Captain Florence, making her do all the work. 'When I'm finished here, that's where we should go.'

'Yeah, all right,' said Martha. She glanced round. The badgers watched in rapt silence. The Doctor's quick and nimble movements simply made their captain seem old and slow and stupid. Again, Martha could see their badger brains struggling to make sense of this challenge to everything they'd been brought up to believe. The kind of reaction most people had when they'd spent five minutes with the Doctor.

'Thing is,' said the Doctor, still moving around inside

the ring of wide-eyed onlookers, 'you should spend a day with the captain of Cleopatra's guard. Taught me all my best moves. And won a medal at the Olympics.' He ducked under Captain Florence's arm as she struck out at him, rolling expertly and leaping back on to his feet. A few of the badgers applauded. Captain Florence glared at them and charged at the Doctor again.

'Oh, very good,' said the Doctor, catching Captain Florence's arm in his, sticking out a leg and tripping her over it. 'You nearly had me there.' The badgers cheered – more than half of them now on the Doctor's side. Jocelyn nudged Martha in the ribs.

'You fancy the Doctor!' she grinned.

'I do not!' Martha protested.

'S'OK,' said Jocelyn. 'I do a bit 'an all.'

Captain Florence and the Doctor faced each other. The Doctor stood tall, calm, his hair hardly even ruffled. The captain bent forward, breathing fast and raggedly, her bristly fur glimmering with sweat. She looked exhausted, and it wasn't just the fight. Martha could see her struggling to cope with being so openly challenged, and the Doctor not showing one iota of fear. It was wearing her down. Martha almost felt sorry for her.

'Tell me if you're getting bored with this,' the Doctor said to Captain Florence. 'And we can do something else.'

'Varmint!' roared Captain Florence and charged at him. They grappled, their arms locked together, the captain's jagged dagger just inches from the Doctor's face. He struggled to resist, pushing and twisting to gain purchase, but she clearly had the weight and strength advantage.

Slowly, slowly, the captain forced the dagger closer to the Doctor. Jocelyn grabbed hold of Martha in her excitement and horror. The Doctor strained, gritting his teeth and he struggled to fend off the knife that almost touched him.

And then he suddenly stopped trying. He fell back onto the floor and Captain Florence, who'd been pressing so hard against him, toppled over too. The Doctor rolled quickly out the way and the captain crashed hard into the ground. She let out a terrible cry of pain, making all those watching flinch. The Doctor got to his feet, the dagger still in his hand.

'Don't we stop for orange squash at some point?' he said, not quite as lightly as before. He wiped the sweat from his forehead on the back of his sleeve.

Some of the badgers gasped. Martha turned to look as Captain Florence rolled roughly over onto her back. The captain grunted, struggled to catch her breath. Her own dagger protruded from her chest, the collarless blouse she wore already stained with blood.

The Doctor ran forward. 'I can help,' he said. But she slapped him hard with the back of her paw and sent him reeling backwards. He lay, amazed, his hand up to his cheek.

Captain Florence got unsteadily to her feet. She shook off the badgers trying to assist her. Martha could see the dagger had gone in deep. And that there was little any of them would be able to do to save her.

'You win the duel,' said Captain Florence, her voice rough and ragged with exertion.

'Let's call it a draw,' said the Doctor from where he lay.

'Hah,' said Captain Florence. 'Good plan.' And she lunged for one of the badgers stood beside her, and snatched her heavy gun.

'Thanks Isobel,' said the captain.

'Er,' said Isobel, terrified. 'S'OK.'

Captain Florence jabbed the gun towards the Doctor, her eyelids flickering as she fought to stay conscious. 'You can live,' she told the Doctor, 'if you come 'ere an' kiss my boots.'

The Doctor gaped at her. He straightened his tie, then looked up at Martha.

'Do it,' Martha told him. 'Please.'

He grinned at her. 'What time do you make it?' he asked.

The question completely threw her. 'What?' she said. 'Doctor, she'll kill you!'

'Oh yeah,' said the Doctor. 'She'll probably do it anyway. I just wanted to know the time.'

Despite everything, Martha glanced down at her watch. 'Nearly half four in the morning,' she said.

The Doctor nodded. 'How nearly?' he said.

'Twenty-eight minutes past,' she told him.

'Right,' said the Doctor. He got slowly to his feet,

brushed himself down and then looked up at Captain Florence. 'You can't win,' he told her. 'Your pirates have had a glimpse of another life, and that'll never go away. Your clients are going to kill you if you go back to them. And you seem to have a dagger sticking out your front.'

'Can,' said Captain Florence. 'Can. Still. Kill. You.'

'Yes you can,' said the Doctor. 'But didn't I say? If you strike me down, I shall become more powerful than you could possibly imagine.'

'Doctor!' said Martha. She could see that the dying captain had nothing left to lose.

The Doctor turned to her and grinned. 'I always wanted to say that. Don't worry, Martha, it's all going to be fine. Really – all going to be fine.' He turned back to Captain Florence. 'I can help you, if you'll let me. Show you a better way of living. What do you say?'

Captain Florence stood, blood pouring from her wound, and it looked like she was considering. Then she shrugged.

'Nah,' she said, and shot him.

Martha screamed, running forward. Captain Florence fell backwards, her body limp. And the Doctor stood quite calmly as the pink light consumed him.

'All right, dear?' said a voice he recognised. The Doctor opened his eyes to see a cartoon sheep smiling back at him. It had been drawn on the side of a chipped mug of tea, which was being held in front of his face. He struggled to sit up and gladly took the tea.

'Thank you,' he said. He found himself in the alleyway between the huge and noisy machines of the engine rooms. The TARDIS stood in the space where it had first materialised, and in front of it stood several of his friends. Mrs Wingsworth had handed him the tea. Behind her stood Archibald and Dashiel and several mouthless men. Archibald waved. The Doctor grinned back at him, at them all.

'Well,' he said. 'That's a relief. I wasn't sure that would really work!'

SIXTEEN

The badgers stood in silence, not sure what to do. Martha stared fixedly at the spot where the Doctor had died, the pink light having eaten him up entirely. She felt nothing, nothing at all. She was dimly aware of a hairy paw taking her hand, of Jocelyn saying something to her. She was dimly aware of hot tears scoring down her cheek. She was dimly aware that nothing mattered any more.

'Right,' said Stanley the badger pirate. 'I'm captain now.' None of the other badger pirates protested. He leered at them. 'An' that means you do what I say!' he roared. A few of the badgers nodded. 'Good,' said Stanley. 'Now, we're gonna shoot these two.'

Martha and Jocelyn were pushed forward into the open space where the Doctor and Captain Florence had fought. Stanley raised his gun at them, then lowered it again.

'Nah,' he said. 'I don't do the shooting. I just give the

order. Isobel! You can shoot 'em.'

'Er,' said the badger pirate Isobel. 'Captain Florence took my gun.'

'Huh,' said Stanley. 'Right. Ruby Tulip. You can shoot 'em.'

A small badger woman with wide and lustrous eyes stepped forward. She raised her gun.

'Er,' she said. 'Which one first?'

Stanley scratched his hairy face with a paw. Then he ip-dipped between Martha and Jocelyn. And chose Martha to die first.

'I'm not scared of you,' she told him.

'Yeah,' he said, awkwardly.

'You just killed the one person who could have changed your lives,' she said.

'Yeah,' said Stanley. 'We kinda know that.' He nodded to Ruby Tulip. Martha braced herself, determined not to scream. And Ruby Tulip pulled the trigger.

Nothing happened. Ruby Tulip stared at her gun, shook it around a bit, and tried again. Nothing happened.

'Gotta do everythin' myself,' muttered Stanley, and he raised his gun at Martha. Nothing happened. 'Er,' he said.

He glanced round at the other badgers, and those with guns tried to shoot Martha. Nothing happened. Jocelyn ran to Martha and threw her arms around her, so hard it almost winded her.

'We're gonna be OK!' said Jocelyn.

'Er,' said Martha, utterly baffled. 'Yeah, I think we are.'

'Wha's goin' on?' snarled Stanley, thumping his gun against the floor and trying to get it to shoot.

'An' where's the captain's body?' asked Isobel beside him.

They all turned to look. Captain Florence had lain at their feet, the dagger protruding from her chest. And now there wasn't even any blood on the floor.

Martha felt something turning over in her stomach. A sudden rush of excitement. They were still stuck in the time loop! 'Look,' she told the badgers, pointing to the great bay window that looked out into the vacuum of space.

Space crackled with pink and blue energy. The pink and blue began to swirl like a whirlpool, getting ever brighter. The badgers shielded their eyes as it exploded white. And from the ball of white light, crackling with pink and pale blue lightning, emerged the Starship *Brilliant*.

Its solar sails glittered silver, the hull and the long fin hanging underneath it sparkling in the starlight. There were no red jelly blotches along it – there was no sign of any damage at all. It was pristine, perfect, good as new. And that could only mean one thing...

'Allo, allo, allo!' called a voice from all around them. 'This is the good ship *Brilliant*. Can someone say something back?'

'Doctor!' laughed Martha, recognising his voice.

'You're alive.'

'Oh yeah,' he said back to her. 'Never been better. Told you it'd all be fine. In fact, we're all fine over here. Having a bit of a party. Hope you weren't worried.'

'Course not,' she lied. 'Anyway, I thought you said you were going to get us out of the time loop.'

'Well, yeah,' he admitted. 'And then I had this better idea.'

'So you made the time loop bigger so that it included the pirate ship.'

'I suppose I did,' said the Doctor. 'Now, there's canapés for everyone over here. Think your badger friends might like to join us? See you in a bit!' And the line to the *Brilliant* went dead.

The badgers all round Martha began to murmur to each other. Stanley threw his gun to the ground at his feet, and there was sudden silence.

'I give the orders!' he yelled.

'Er,' said the badger woman, Zuzia. 'Can we go to the party?' She furrowed her hairy forehead as a thought came slowly to her. 'Please,' she added.

'No!' shouted Stanley. 'I'm in charge! I'm the captain!'

The badgers shuddered with fear of him. But Kitty Rose raised a paw nervously.

'What?' snapped Stanley.

'Er,' said Kitty Rose, with all the other badgers looking at her. 'What can you do to stop us jus' going?'

Stanley's jaw dropped open in amazement at the very idea. And in the moment that he didn't say anything, that he didn't shout her down or lunge at her, the other badgers knew the answer. They dropped their guns, they laughed and cheered, and hurried away to the lifts.

Martha, Jocelyn and Stanley stood alone together in front of the great bay window. Tiny capsules were already zipping away from the pirate ship and they watched them clustering round the *Brilliant*. A bay door opened in the side of the starship and the capsules queued up in an orderly fashion to be allowed aboard.

'You should come with us,' said Martha to Stanley, and put her hand on his shoulder. 'Join the party.'

'Huh,' said Stanley, shaking her hand away.

'She's right,' said a voice that Martha thought for a moment belonged to Jocelyn. They turned to see Captain Florence walking down from between the passageway of hanging silks. Her collarless blouse was torn and bloodstained, but otherwise she looked just fine.

'Captain,' said Stanley quietly, knowing his brief time as boss was now over.

Martha gazed at the captain. 'You can't do anything to hurt us now,' she said.

'Yeah,' said Captain Florence. 'Can't beat ya. Might as well come to this 'ere party.'

Martha, Captain Florence, Jocelyn and Stanley made their way to the lift. As it took them down to the hangars where the capsules awaited, Captain Florence turned to Martha.

'The canner-peas,' she said quietly. 'You're gonna 'ave to show me what to do.'

Martha grinned at her. 'Don't worry,' she said. 'Everything's going to be fine.'

Music played all through the *Brilliant*, lively, poppy stuff. On the bridge and in the passageways, the Balumin taught badger pirates how to dance. Captain Georgina, Thomas and the rest of the human crew were no better at the complex dance steps. Gabriel and the other robots tried to serve drinks and nibbles but got grabbed by the dancers and made to join in.

Martha made her way through the laughing, chatting, dancing party and headed for the cocktail lounge. Mrs Wingsworth was regaling Dashiel with tales of her adventures aboard the pirate ship, and he tried not to be rude about getting up when Jocelyn walked into the room. Martha watched Mrs Wingsworth gape in astonishment at such terrible manners, then turn to the badger woman sat next to her and continue with her story.

The Doctor stood behind the bar, busy making milkshakes. 'Martha!' he said.

'Hiya!' she said, sitting on one the tall bar stools. He handed her a glass of pink and yellow milkshake.

'Haven't done this in ages,' he said. 'And they've got really good ice cream!'

She was happy just to sit there and let him make drinks for everybody. The party tumbled all around her, wild and mad and fun. And far too full of different people.

'The *Brilliant*,' she said to the Doctor. 'You made it bigger on the inside.'

'Well,' admitted the Doctor, scraping chocolate sprinkles onto six milkshakes all at once. 'A bit. The maths works out. If you're not using time, you can stretch space around.'

'Right,' she said, not needing to understand him. 'And you're gonna tell me how you made their guns stop working?'

'That was good, wasn't it?' said the Doctor. 'I left a note for Gabriel earlier. Said the guns were being used on the passengers, and wouldn't it be better if their power was used for something else.'

'So when the *Brilliant* came back it used the power in the guns?' said Martha.

'Aw,' said the Doctor. 'There's only a tiny bit of power in a gun. So it didn't *need* the extra energy. But since the *Brilliant* was warping stuff anyway, it seemed like a good idea.'

'Right,' said Martha. 'And you didn't break us out of the loop. You just extended it.'

'Yeah,' said the Doctor. 'I was in the TARDIS and the problem wasn't to get us *out* of the time loop, it was fixing the gap. Which the TARDIS could do with a little bit of effort, warping space and time a bit until things lined up nicely. Soon as you hit a point where the numbers balance out, the loop takes over for itself. And while I was at it I extended the loop so it lassoed the pirate ship in with us. So we're in it, the pirate ship's in it and so's everything in between. And now it's a complete loop, it will just run and run for ever.'

'But there was a delay,' said Martha. 'Before, people came back if you just looked away.'

'Yeah,' said the Doctor. 'That's because the loop was broken and the *Brilliant* was always trying to fix it. Now if they die or they run out of canapés they'll all come back in one go. Every hour or so.'

'Which is why you wanted to know the time,' she said.

'Yeah,' said the Doctor. 'We were just coming up to the end of the hour when Captain Florence shot me. Another few minutes and I'd have had to wait for the next go round. Which would have looked less clever. Now. Make yourself useful.'

He had loaded a tray with tall glasses of milkshake, each glass festooned with straws and paper umbrellas. She gathered up the tray carefully and he pointed to the table of mouthless men in leather aprons and Bermuda shorts, all looking slightly uneasy. She guessed that, like the badgers, they'd never been invited to parties.

While the mouthless men drank their milkshakes – using the straws provided – Martha watched Archibald giving lessons to other badgers on which canapés were best. She went to join them, kissed Archibald on his hairy cheek, and took one of the cheese and pineapple sticks from him.

He grinned at her. 'This is Toby,' he said. 'An' Oliver and Patrick. They're learnin' about blinis.'

Martha shook the paws of the three badgers, then nodded at the female badgers who watched her with fascination. 'Who are the girls?' she asked Archibald.

'Er,' said Archibald coyly. 'Tha's Zuzia and Kitty Rose,' he said. 'They don't say much. They jus' watch us and whisper.'

Martha watched Zuzia and Kitty Rose whisper to one another, and then giggle like teenage girls. Archibald, she realised, was something of a hit.

SEVENTEEN

Later, Martha's watch said three in the afternoon but it felt like late at night, maybe even into the next day. She had fallen over while teaching the badgers how to do the Conga, she had slow-danced with Archibald and then surrendered him to Zuzia, and she'd been the Doctor's assistant when he'd done card tricks in the cabaret. All in all, she was exhausted. So she sat in the cocktail lounge, sipping her hydrogen hydroxide and watching everyone else enjoy the party.

The Doctor slumped down in the chair beside her, a stupid grin on his face. 'Isn't this...' he gestured at the happy throng of tentacled Balumin, badger-faced former pirates, mouthless men from the engine room and the rest of the starship's crew. 'Isn't it just...' But he couldn't quite think of the word.

'Brilliant?' Martha suggested.

'Yeah!' said the Doctor laughing. 'That's exactly what this is.'

'You want to stay, do you?'

His grin faded, and in his eyes there was that terrible alien loneliness. He tried not to show it when he turned to her. 'Nah,' he said, all false cheer and ease. 'We'd get bored. Well, I'd get bored. And that'd be boring for you. So yeah, we'd both get bored. What I said the first time.'

'Doctor,' she said seriously. 'What about everyone else?'

'What about them?'

'They might get bored, too?'

'What?' he said. 'On a ship with everlasting cheese and pineapple on sticks?'

Martha held his gaze, saying nothing. She knew he knew better than that. It was just that sometimes he needed reminding.

'OK,' he said at length and got to his feet. Then he climbed unsteadily onto the chair beside her, and started clapping his hands. 'Attention!' he called. 'Oi, you 'orrible lot, lend me your ears!'

The noise of the party died down and people came in from the ballroom to hear what he had to say.

'Speech!' called Mrs Wingsworth.

'Speech!' agreed Captain Georgina, who looked a little tipsy and was wearing a paper hat.

'Speech!' joined in the rest of the party. The Doctor let them work themselves up a bit before calling for some quiet.

'All right, a speech,' he said, and earned a massive cheer. 'The party here never ends,' he said – again a massive cheer. 'And there's nobody who can tell you otherwise,' he went on. And then, after a dramatic pause, he added, 'except you.'

The party-goers glanced round at each other nervously, not sure what the Doctor meant.

'Me and Martha,' he told them. 'We're leaving. In an hour.'

The audience booed good-naturedly.

'And when we're gone,' said the Doctor, 'that's it. There's no way out of here. You stay here for ever.'

The background rumble of chatter died suddenly away. Everyone stood transfixed by the Doctor.

'So,' he told them. 'You can come with us. We'll drop you off somewhere, and you continue your lives as you were. With a war coming. With real stuff to deal with. With food that runs out and people who die and things never quite the same any more.'

He let them take that in. 'Or you can stay. For ever. The party going on and on, never getting old. But it never being any different. Never getting outside. Never seeing anyone else. But safe.'

They hung on the words, awed by what he was saying. 'No one owns any of you. No one else gets to decide. You each have to make your own choice. My ship's the blue box in the engine rooms,' he said. 'You've got an hour to decide. Come on, Martha.'

He jumped down from the chair, took Martha's hand in his and led her through the crowd. The party-goers gaped at them in silence, the only sound coming from the *Brilliant*'s hidden speakers as a pop tune came to an end.

Martha let the Doctor lead her to the centre of the ballroom, the passengers and pirates and crew all around them. The Doctor took Martha's left hand in his, put his right hand on her waist. Realising what he meant to do, she put her hand to his shoulder, so close to him she could feel the buttons of his suit against her chest, so close she could feel his hearts beating.

'But what if they want to stay?' she asked him, looking around at the various friends they had made and those she'd not even got to know.

'Then they stay,' said the Doctor. 'But they have to choose.'

From the *Brilliant*'s speakers, a new pop song began. It took a moment for Martha to realise what it was, by which time she and the Doctor had already started dancing.

'Grace Kelly!' she laughed.

'The song,' the Doctor nodded, wheeling her around the floor. 'Got it off your iPod. Thought you wouldn't mind. Good old Mika.'

Following the Doctor and Martha's lead, others joined the dance floor: Jocelyn and Dashiel; Thomas and Captain Florence; Mrs Wingsworth and one of the mouthless men; Archibald and *both* Kitty Rose and Zuzia. Martha could see the same look on all their faces; the same determination to enjoy themselves, the same terror and confusion as they tried to make their choices.

Martha looked away quickly, torn on their behalf. She kept her mind on the music and not treading on the Doctor's toes. At least she didn't have to make that choice herself, she thought. But really she already had, a long time ago. And one day he'd take her back to her own time, and she'd have to choose again...

She hung on to the Doctor and let him lead.

The party aboard the *Brilliant* would go on for ever. Yet for those who would choose the one chance to escape, the last dance had begun.

Acknowledgements

Thanks to Justin and Gary for thinking of me in the first place, and to all those people who listened to my odd ideas and answered my odd questions. Special mention to the experts Scott Andrews, Simon Belcher, Debbie Challis, Richard Flowers, Tim Guerrier, Tom Guerrier, Danny Kodicek, Joseph Lidster, Amanda Lindsay, Nicholas Pegg, Steve Tribe and Alex Wilcock. The best bits are probably theirs.

Thanks also to my pals at Big Finish for all they've let me get away with recently.

And lastly thanks to my nephews, Luke and Joseph, to whom the badger-faced pirates owe something of a debt.

Also available from BBC Books
featuring the Doctor and Rose
as played by David Tennant and Billie Piper:

DOCTOR·WHO

THE STONE ROSE
by Jacqueline Rayner

THE FEAST OF THE DROWNED
by Stephen Cole

THE RESURRECTION CASKET
by Justin Richards

THE NIGHTMARE OF BLACK ISLAND
by Mike Tucker

THE ART OF DESTRUCTION
by Stephen Cole

THE PRICE OF PARADISE
by Colin Brake

DOCTOR · WHO

Sting of the Zygons

by Stephen Cole

ISBN 978 1 84607 225 3

UK £6.99 US $11.99/$14.99 CDN

The TARDIS lands the Doctor and Martha in the Lake District in 1909, where a small village has been terrorised by a giant, scaly monster. The search is on for the elusive 'Beast of Westmorland', and explorers, naturalists and hunters from across the country are descending on the fells. King Edward VII himself is on his way to join the search, with a knighthood for whoever finds the Beast.

But there is a more sinister presence at work in the Lakes than a mere monster on the rampage, and the Doctor is soon embroiled in the plans of an old and terrifying enemy. As the hunters become the hunted, a desperate battle of wits begins – with the future of the entire world at stake…

The Last Dodo

by Jacqueline Rayner

ISBN 978 1 84607 224 6

UK £6.99 US $11.99/$14.99 CDN

The Doctor and Martha go in search of a real live dodo,
and are transported by the TARDIS to the mysterious
Museum of the Last Ones. There, in the Earth section,
they discover every extinct creature up to the present
day, all still alive and in suspended animation.

Preservation is the museum's only job – collecting
the last of every endangered species from all over the
universe. But exhibits are going missing…

Can the Doctor solve the mystery before the museum's
curator adds the last of the Time Lords to her
collection?

Also available from BBC Books
featuring the Doctor and Martha
as played by David Tennant and Freema Agyeman:

DOCTOR · WHO

Forever Autumn
by Mark Morris
ISBN 978 1 84607 270 3
UK £6.99 US $11.99/$14.99 CDN

It is almost Halloween in the sleepy New England
town of Blackwood Falls. Autumn leaves litter lawns
and sidewalks, paper skeletons hang in windows, and
carved pumpkins leer from stoops and front porches.

The Doctor and Martha soon discover that something
long dormant has awoken in the town, and this will
be no ordinary Halloween. What is the secret of the
ancient tree and the mysterious book discovered
tangled in its roots? What rises from the local
churchyard in the dead of night, sealing up the lips of
the only witness? And why are the harmless trappings
of Halloween suddenly taking on a creepy new life of
their own?

As nightmarish creatures prowl the streets, the
Doctor and Martha must battle to prevent both the
townspeople and themselves from suffering a grisly
fate…

Also available from BBC Books
featuring the Doctor and Martha
as played by David Tennant and Freema Agyeman:

DOCTOR·WHO

Sick Building

by Paul Magrs

ISBN 978 1 84607 269 7

UK £6.99 US $11.99/$14.99 CDN

Tiermann's World: a planet covered in wintry woods and roamed by sabre-toothed tigers and other savage beasts. The Doctor is here to warn Professor Tiermann, his wife and their son that a terrible danger is on its way.

The Tiermanns live in luxury, in a fantastic, futuristic, fully automated Dreamhome, under an impenetrable force shield. But that won't protect them from the Voracious Craw. A gigantic and extremely hungry alien creature is heading remorselessly towards their home. When it gets there everything will be devoured.

Can they get away in time? With the force shield cracking up, and the Dreamhome itself deciding who should or should not leave, things are looking desperate…

When the TARDIS makes a disastrous landing in the swamps of the planet Sunday, the Doctor has no choice but to abandon Martha and try to find help. But the tranquillity of Sunday's swamps is deceptive, and even the TARDIS can't protect Martha forever.

The human pioneers of Sunday have their own dangers to face: homeless and alone, they're only just starting to realise that Sunday's wildlife isn't as harmless as it first seems. Why are the native otters behaving so strangely, and what is the creature in the swamps that is so interested in the humans, and the new arrivals?

The Doctor and Martha must fight to ensure that human intelligence doesn't become the greatest danger of all.

Also available from BBC Books
featuring the Doctor and Martha
as played by David Tennant and Freema Agyeman:

DOCTOR · WHO

Wishing Well

by Trevor Baxendale
ISBN 978 1 84607 348 9
UK £6.99 US $11.99/$14.99 CDN

The old village well is just a curiosity – something to attract tourists intrigued by stories of lost treasure, or visitors just making a wish. Unless something alien and terrifying could be lurking inside the well? Something utterly monstrous that causes nothing but death and destruction?

But who knows the real truth about the well? Who wishes to unleash the hideous force it contains? What terrible consequences will follow the search for a legendary treasure hidden at the bottom?

No one wants to believe the Doctor's warnings about the deadly horror lying in wait – but soon they'll wish they had…

Also available from BBC Books
featuring the Doctor and Martha
as played by David Tennant and Freema Agyeman:

DOCTOR·WHO

Peacemaker
by James Swallow
ISBN 978 1 84607 349 6
UK £6.99 US $11.99/$14.99 CDN

The peace and quiet of a remote homestead in the
1880s American West is shattered by the arrival of two
shadowy outriders searching for 'the healer'. When the
farmer refuses to help them, they raze the house to the
ground using guns that shoot bolts of energy instead of
bullets...

In the town of Redwater, the Doctor and Martha
learn of a snake-oil salesman whose patent medicines
actually cure his patient. But when the Doctor and
Martha investigate they discover the truth is stranger,
and far more dangerous.

Caught between the law of the gun and the deadly
plans of intergalactic mercenaries, the Doctor and
Martha are about to discover just how wild the West
can become...

DOCTOR·WHO
The Inside Story
by Gary Russell
ISBN 978 0 56348 649 7
£14.99

In March 2005, a 900-year-old alien in a police public
call box made a triumphant return to our television
screens. *The Inside Story* takes us behind the scenes to
find out how the series was commissioned, made and
brought into the twenty-first century. Gary Russell has
talked extensively to everyone involved in the show,
from the Tenth Doctor himself, David Tennant, and
executive producer Russell T Davies, to the people
normally hidden inside monster suits or behind
cameras. Everyone has an interesting story to tell.

The result is the definitive account of how the new
Doctor Who was created. With exclusive access to design
drawings, backstage photographs, costume designs and
other previously unpublished pictures, *The Inside Story*
covers the making of all twenty-six episodes of Series
One and Two, plus the Christmas specials, as well as an
exclusive look ahead to the third series.

DOCTOR·WHO

Creatures and Demons

by Justin Richards

ISBN 978 1 84607 229 1
UK £7.99 US $12.99/$15.99 CDN

Throughout his many adventures in time and space, the Doctor has encountered aliens, monsters, creatures and demons from right across the universe. In this third volume of alien monstrosities and dastardly villains, *Doctor Who* expert and acclaimed author Justin Richards describes some of the evils the Doctor has fought in over forty years of time travel.

From the grotesque Abzorbaloff to the monstrous Empress of the Racnoss, from giant maggots to the Daleks of the secret Cult of Skaro, from the Destroyer of Worlds to the ancient Beast itself… This book brings together more of the terrifying enemies the Doctor has battled against.

Illustrated throughout with stunning photographs and design drawings from the current series of *Doctor Who* and his previous 'classic' incarnations, this book is a treat for friends of the Doctor whatever their age, and whatever planet they come from…

Coming soon from *BBC Books*:

DOCTOR · WHO

Starships and Spacestations

by Justin Richards

ISBN 978 1 84607 423 3

£7.99 US $12.99/$15.99 CDN

The Doctor has his TARDIS to get him from place to place and time to time, but the rest of the Universe relies on more conventional transport… From the British Space Programme of the late twentieth century to Earth's Empire in the far future, from the terrifying Dalek Fleet to deadly Cyber Ships, this book documents the many starships and spacestations that the Doctor and his companions have encountered on their travels.

He has been held prisoner in space, escaped from the moon, witnessed the arrival of the Sycorax and the crash landing of a space pig… More than anyone else, the Doctor has seen the development of space travel between countless worlds.

This stunningly illustrated book tells the amazing story of Earth's ventures into space, examines the many alien fleets who have paid Earth a visit, and explores the other starships and spacestations that the Doctor has encountered on his many travels…